The
DEVIL'S
SPAWN

The
DEVIL'S
SPAWN

USA TODAY BESTSELLING AUTHOR
GEMMA JAMES

Note To Readers

The Devil's Spawn is a dark romance with a BDSM edge that does NOT conform to safe, sane, and consensual practices. Includes explicit content and subject matter that may offend some readers. Intended for mature audiences. Book four in the *Devil's Kiss* series.

1. IMPETUOUS

Present - 1 day before Thanksgiving

I will not fucking cry.

"Damn it," I muttered as a tear escaped. Gritting my teeth, I blinked rapidly and stuffed more clothing into the overflowing suitcase. An absurd amount of dresses rose above the rim, and as I shoved the pile down, I wished like hell I had some pants. Or even a few pairs of sweats. Definitely some underwear. But those finer things in life weren't allowed—not when it meant blocking my husband's access to his favorite place between my thighs.

I wrestled with the zipper, adding my body weight to the top of the case, and finally zipped it shut. If I walked out that door, I'd have nothing but what lay in a tossed mess inside. The remainder of my clothing filled the shelves, drawers, and hangers inside the walk-in wardrobe I shared with Gage.

Oh, God…Eve.

How was I supposed to tell her? She'd miss her

bedroom, her toys. She'd miss *him*.

The reality of what I was doing hit me, and in a fit of anger, I dragged the suitcase off the bed and kicked the damned thing until it fell over on its side. Okay, so I wasn't exactly thinking logically, but didn't a pregnant woman have the right to a meltdown after finding out her husband was nothing but a lying—

Don't go there.

But I went there anyway, torturing myself with every word the bitch had spoken. Nearly doubling over at the thought, I pressed a desperate fist to my lips and stifled a sob; sucked in quick breaths before letting them out in hot spurts that dampened my knuckles. Where had the tears come from? I'd promised myself I wouldn't cry anymore.

Pull it together, Kayla.

He was due to arrive in the driveway any minute now. Simone had begged me to leave before he got home, but if I were going to do this, I had to confront him first. Otherwise, he would never let me go. A hand dropped onto my shoulder, warm with comforting support. Simone didn't say a word, but she didn't need to. I knew she wouldn't leave my side, and that's why I'd called her. She was my safety net, the one person who wouldn't hesitate to hand Gage his ass if he tried railroading me. She was here to make sure I got out.

"You don't owe him anything," she said.

Nodding, I wiped my eyes. "I know."

I didn't know shit. My husband was the fucking devil incarnate, but he loved me. Didn't he? Or had it all been a lie? That was the problem—I didn't know anymore. My emotions had me trapped in the eye of a typhoon named Gage Channing.

Simone's hand slid from my shoulder as I rebuilt my emotional fortress. I stood to the side in bitter numbness while she hauled my suitcase upright. She headed toward the bedroom door, rollers sounding on the hardwood behind her.

"It's okay to need some space, you know. If he loves you, he'll understand."

Folding my arms, I sank onto the end of the mattress. This particular spot bled with memories. He'd bend me over in a heartbeat and blast some sense into my ass if I let him. I couldn't let him get that close, or I'd crack wide open. Hell, I'd probably fracture regardless.

"I need to do this," I said, shaking my head just as his car sounded. "I need some space, but I also need…"

Answers.

Simone lingered by the bedroom door, chewing her bottom lip. Uncertainty was a strange feature on her face. She didn't do uncertain—she was a pick-a-path-and-follow-it kind of woman.

"I'll be okay, Simone. I promise."

She let out a sigh. "I'll be right out there," she said, jabbing a finger in the direction of the living room. She left the door cracked open upon her exit, and her absence echoed in my ears. The room hummed a solitary tune, and each lonesome note poked at my will. But a single question repeated on loop within the chaos of my foggy mind. Could I really go through with this?

2. UNDER DURESS

Past - 18 days before Halloween

I was going to be sick. The inevitability of it sat in the back of my throat, burning like acid. My stomach cramped, and a sweaty chill broke out on my skin. I wasn't immune to the irony in that, but it was true.

As I watched Katherine trail a manicured hand down Gage's arm, I seethed hot and cold, raged with clammy sickness. I lifted a hand, a millisecond away from shoving his office door all the way open, but his harsh voice made me freeze.

"Get your hands off of me."

Katherine jerked back as if he'd burned her, and only then did I realize that I'd seen her touching him for maybe two seconds.

But two seconds had been enough to make me sick. Literally sick. Before Gage or Katherine spotted me, and before anyone on this floor questioned why I was lingering outside my husband's office, I strode toward the women's restroom, my head held high with false confidence. Hopefully, anyone looking at me wouldn't see the truth on my face.

That I'd caught him with her *again*, and I was about to come undone over it.

A phone rang, fingers clicked over a keyboard, and I heard the distinct scratching of someone jabbing down quick and purposeful notes with a pencil. I held my shit together long enough to reach the safety of the ladies room. Thank God it was empty. I scurried to my knees in one of the stalls and lost my pride along with my breakfast.

He'd told me to meet him for lunch. Why would he do that if Katherine was going to be here? He knew how the sight of that bitch got under my skin. Gage had a sadistic streak as black as the desert at midnight, but when it came to Katherine Mitchell, he exercised care. In fact, he went out of his way to spare me her presence.

Because he was fucking her? Or because he loved me enough to shield me from her?

I hated how she was the weak spot in my armor, the single chink that made the rest of me fall apart. I didn't want to doubt him, but the image of her four months ago in the basement, eager and on her knees, was a searing brand on my memory. It didn't matter that he'd only threatened to follow through to make a point, to show me what *could* be if I dared to betray him again.

The mental damage had been done.

Tears stung my eyes. Damn, I had to get my shit

together. I couldn't go back out there and face the employees of Channing Enterprises—face *him*—looking like I'd just had a breakdown in the women's restroom. Even if that was kind of true. Turning the faucet on, I shot my reflection a stern frown then splashed cold water onto my face.

Five minutes later, I left the restroom mostly composed. As always, the curious gazes of my former coworkers burned into my back. I didn't check to see if they were watching me, but I felt it. Maybe I was paranoid, though I didn't think so. My marriage to CEO Gage Channing was a cesspool for gossip mongers, especially since Katherine and her son had come into our lives. The selfish, jealous wife in me wanted to keep Conner at arm's length, but he was just a kid, and he had the best parts of Gage in him, so much so that I found it shocking his paternity hadn't come out sooner.

Not for the first time, I wondered why Katherine had waited so long to tell Gage about Conner. Maybe marrying me had been the final push that sent her over the edge. Maybe she'd always believed Gage to be hers, so coming clean about a secret like that hadn't seemed important. Maybe the idea of coming clean had even scared her—until another woman had taken him away and that had scared her more.

Well, the bitch couldn't have him. And speaking of Katherine, she was thankfully nowhere in sight when I entered his office.

"You're late," he said, dark head bowed toward the screen of his laptop.

I shut and locked the door. "I know. I'm sorry." I crossed to the front of his executive desk and bent over, lifting my skirt as I did so. I could explain how seeing Katherine had caught me off guard, but I didn't want to stir that pot right now, and I definitely didn't want to go into how I'd puked in the women's restroom, even if telling him might spare me a punishment.

He might think it meant something else, and with a stab to the heart, I acknowledged once again that it wasn't going to happen. Not after all of this time. We'd been married for over a year and a half now, screwing like rabbits the whole time without any form of protection, yet I continued to be…broken.

The painful reminder of that almost drowned me in despair until the texture of his suit against my outer thigh pulled me from my dark thoughts. I bit my lip as he grabbed my ass with a warm palm. He wasn't gentle, and the rough way he handled me made my insides clench in the best way imaginable. Anticipation zinged through me as I waited for his punishment. I had no doubt he was going to spank me for arriving late, but he knew what the heat of his palm on my bare ass did to me, so calling it a form of discipline was a stretch.

"I can practically hear the wheels turning in your head. What's on your mind?" he asked.

I gnawed on my bottom lip some more and considered what to tell him. What not to tell him. "I'm thinking of how turned on I am."

"Are you aching for my hand? Is that why you were late?"

I groaned. "No."

"I'm going to need a little clarification."

"I wasn't late on purpose." A dark note entered my tone, and I hoped he didn't pick up on it.

"But you'll take a spanking for it anyway?"

I nodded.

"Fuck," he groaned. "You've got me so damn hard." He smacked my ass to punctuate just how hard he was. "Spread your legs."

I gripped my skirt and did as told, exposing myself to the gentle caress of air on my pussy. The remnants of Katherine and her whorish fingers vanished from my mind. There was nothing but wet heat between my legs. I ached for him there. Tingled. Burned.

He'd been away at a conference for a few days and had gotten back late last night. I'd already gone to bed, and instead of waking me to claim what was his, he'd shown a rare bout of sweetness by letting me sleep. But going so long without his cock was beginning to drive me insane.

He trailed a finger between my butt cheeks, drawing a surprised gasp from me. "I need you," I moaned.

My words gave him pause, and his touch lingered but did little more. God, he could be such a tease.

"Please."

Finally, he touched me exactly how I wanted...no, *needed* with his thumb teasing my asshole while two fingers slipped inside me.

I moaned at the welcome intrusion. "Feels so good."

"I'm going to spank the fuck out of this ass."

And he did. He walloped me with more force than I expected, considering his playful mood. I gritted my teeth to keep quiet, dancing from foot to foot between each hit, but on his final, most brutal strike I failed to bite back a yelp.

He palmed my right ass cheek and squeezed. "Beautifully pink."

My legs were rigid pillars of steel, driven wide open by the strength of my need for his cock. "Please," I said, groaning the word. I fisted my skirt to keep from touching myself.

"Shhh," he said, shoving his fingers between my lips. "I have other uses for this mouth. Do you have any idea how badly I want you gagging on my cock? I've thought of nothing else but getting into your mouth and ass since I've been gone."

My heartbeat stuttered, and I would have begged for mercy if he'd given me a chance. Instead, I moaned my protest around his fingers. He understood exactly what I was objecting to.

"I've gone easy on you, but you've grown spoiled. Entitled even. I own your ass. We agreed on our anniversary that it's mine to take as I please." Leaning against my back, he pressed his erection into my ass cheek and brought his lips to my ear. "I *please*," he said.

I bit down on his fingers in response, instinctively clenching my ass at the thought of him shoving his cock inside. Abruptly, he sprang back. Turning to face him, I gripped his desk behind me.

"Not here, Gage. Please."

He gestured to his desk, eyes smoldering. "Bare your cunt."

Oh hell. I was a pile of goo at his feet, sculpting clay in his strong hands. I hopped up, bunched my skirt around my waist, and spread for him much too eagerly. Propping myself up on my elbows, I watched him as he inched closer with that burning indigo gaze zeroing in between my thighs.

Hot energy blazed between us, and exhilaration squeezed my heart, rushed through my veins.

Then he smiled and asked his favorite question. "Who am I?"

"My Master."

"Always, Kayla." He dropped to his knees and placed his hands on my thighs, his thumbs digging into my skin as he spread me even wider. He wet his lips with a furtive dart of his tongue. "Who decides when you come?"

"You do, Master."

Please, please, please, please. I need to come. So fucking ba—

"I've decided you're not coming." He shot me his devil's grin. "But I'm going to lick you right here on my desk until you beg me to."

I almost cried at his words. Defeated, I closed my eyes and let my head fall back, swallowed a frustrated growl. Fuuuck...his breath would be the end of me, drifting over my exposed pussy with enough heat to make my blood rush right *there*. And his tongue...damn, that tongue.

Wet and on fire, sliding between my lips with perfected finesse. Easing through my slickness with lazy purpose, as if he had all day to eat me out. Which, of course, he did. He always had time to torture me.

"You're not leaving here satisfied." Slowly, he inched two expert fingers into my pussy. "You're going to leave my office with pink cheeks, a throbbing cunt, and beyond excited to get fucked in the ass tonight."

I groaned.

"Eyes on me, Kayla."

"Master, I'm begging you." With a roll of my shoulders, I dipped my head, chin to chest, and returned his gaze beneath hooded lids.

He had me gone already. Primed and ready. My nipples puckered to the point of pain, the very tips straining against my bra, begging for freedom from the sheer fabric so he'd fondle them. Lick them. Pinch them.

"There you are," he whispered, crooking his fingers inside me before sliding them in and out. Slooooow. So damn slow.

"Oh God, Gage. Please, please…"

"Will you do anything to come?"

The bastard was trying to trick me again. I bit my lip to keep from answering. If I said yes, he'd take advantage of any number of things. Nipple clamps. A cane or bullwhip. His favorite gag, nearly as big as my fist.

My husband was beyond sadistic. He had no qualms about pushing me past hard limits if I gave him the go ahead, and he'd hold me to my green light even if I gave it while under duress.

"That's not fair."

"The only rules I play by are my own," he said, then

he lowered his mouth to me again.

Nothing could be as erotic as watching him go down on me. Nothing. I reached under my splayed thighs and gripped the edge of the desk with both hands. He'd given me plenty of lessons on the art of limber movement, and right now I used my body's capabilities to grind against his face.

There. God. So close. I was going to come, and I didn't give a fuck about the consequences. He'd find a reason to take his pound of flesh anyway because he was Gage. "Yeah, yeah," I panted, barely above a whisper. "So close."

He jackhammered his fingers a few more times until I writhed on his desk, and then he shot my hopes down the drain by pulling away. "Good. That's exactly where I want you." Wiping his mouth with the back of his hand, he pulled himself upright and towered over me. "I'll see you at home. I won't be late."

The fight went out of me, and I plopped onto his desk, trying to catch my breath. "Don't leave me like this."

"You know what I want, Kayla. Give it to me, and I'll take you there."

He wanted to fuck me in the ass—only he wanted me to give it to him willingly. More than willingly. He wanted me to beg him to take me in the one way he knew I despised. If that wasn't sadistic, then I didn't know what was.

3. SECRET LITTLE NOTES

Awareness could be a cruel thing, especially when it was of one's self. The whisper in my head, an irritating voice that sounded eerily close to my own, chanted vicious truth. I was a sex addict. No. I was a Gage Channing addict. I'd given up the idea of quitting him a long time ago, but tonight, as I set the table and prepared to greet him, I realized just how pathetic I was, how far I'd fallen through the fissures in my sanity.

He'd thrown down the anal gauntlet at the most opportune time—for *him* anyway—when he had me out of my mind and foaming at the mouth from withdrawal. I could think of nothing else since I'd left his office. My head was crammed full of Gage and sex and the pain he'd inevitably inflict. Poor Eve had been dealing with my dazed-like distraction all afternoon. I'd managed to get my head out of my ass long enough to help her with her homework. We spent thirty minutes gathering leaves from the ground, each one a bright shade of autumn splendor. Afterward, I patiently watched her glue them to an outline

13

of a tree on a white piece of paper.

But the glue hadn't even dried before I'd gone back to obsessing over Gage's plans for my ass. Something rose in my throat. Fear? Maybe. I swallowed that bitter lump of emotion as I layered the ingredients for lasagna into a baking dish. It was Gage's favorite, but I guess tonight was all about Gage's favorites, especially anal.

That word had such intensity to it, such power and control. And fear it I did, because anal was so unpredictable. Sometimes it felt good. Unbelievably good. But other times…

Gage was careful, but his definition of careful and mine were two entirely different things. Sometimes his sadism took over and my ass became the casualty. We didn't do it often, and I suspected that was the reason why. Even he didn't quite trust himself. How could he, when he craved my pain on such a fundamental level?

Fifteen minutes before I expected him home, a text pinged my cell. He'd given back my phone a few weeks ago, with parental controls to restrict my access, of course. In addition to emergency contacts, and Eve's school and doctors, I could only call or text him, and vice versa.

Gage: *what's Eve doing?*
Me: *watching tv*
Gage: *did she finish her homework?*
Me: *yep, all done*
Gage: *good, go into the bedroom and touch yourself. I'm checking you when I get home. You'd better be wet.*

I bit back a groan as I tapped out a *yes, Master.*

Gage: *lock the door and get on all fours on the bed. First thing I want to see is your ass in the air. I'll be there in a few.*

Damn him.

Setting my cell on the counter, I eyed the oven and the minutes ticking by. Eve was engrossed in her "TV time," which gave me a chance to slip down the hall and quietly push the bedroom door open.

I couldn't help but love this game that Gage and I played. The rules always changed, and he always won, but the ride was the biggest thrill ever—like sitting white-knuckled at the top of a roller coaster, on the cusp of hurtling down into the unknown. I locked the door, well aware he had a key, and crossed to the bed and got into position. Head down, ass up. I slipped my fingers between my legs and started stroking, going easy because it would take so little to get me there, and that was, under no circumstances, allowed.

I heard his car through the cracked window in our bedroom, followed by footsteps that led him to the front door. Then silence stole over me, save for my rapid pulse. I listened for a hint of him in the hall but detected not a single footfall. Besides, I didn't need to hear or see him to know the exact moment he entered the bedroom.

His presence tingled on my skin, sparking my nerve endings until they sizzled with electricity. My body flushed, and the satin comforter seemed to grow hot under my skin.

He had me boiling already.

"Dinner smells wonderful," he murmured, taking my vulnerable ass in his hands. "According to the timer, we've got six minutes."

"Six minutes for what?" I gulped. He had to notice the shaky quality of my voice. Six minutes wasn't nearly enough time. Not for anal.

"Relax. I'd never rush this. You should know better by now." His clothing rustled, and I heard a cap open, followed by a squirt. "I'm only prepping you with a plug."

I let out a breath. Those weren't so bad. Sometimes, they were even…arousing. He pressed the cold, hard tip against my rectum, but he didn't shove it in right away. Instead, he swirled the plug around my reluctant hole, spreading the lubricant.

He really was taking care with this, but considering my meltdown the last time he fucked me in the backdoor, I shouldn't be surprised. Gage lived to make me submit, and though my pain never failed to harden his cock, he'd come a long way from the monster he'd once been. Either that or I'd trained myself to accept his will because it was easier than fighting him.

He nudged my ass with the plug, and I winced, my body automatically tensing.

"Just relax for me."

I blew out a breath. Easier said than done. He probed my ass more firmly, and this time he didn't hesitate. I didn't dare move away from him, no matter how much I wanted to. It didn't matter that this was the biggest fucking butt plug he'd ever used. It didn't matter that it hurt. If I didn't hold still and take that plug in silent submission, he would punish me into next Sunday. Finally, the horrendous ring of fire abated, leaving in its wake an anus brimming with his toy.

He dragged a finger through my slit. "You are so damn wet. Such a dirty, needy girl." He swatted my ass with enough force to extract a yelp from me. "Take a minute if you need to. I'll get dinner on the table." The soft pad of his feet carried him away from me, and his quiet exit echoed in my ears.

My heartbeat thundered as I made my way into the bathroom. Acclimating to the foreign object in my ass took a few moments, but by the time I'd wiped away the excess lube from between my cheeks, it felt mostly... comfortable.

Not really arousing though, considering the size. But Gage didn't have a small cock, so I understood why he'd chosen this one.

I turned toward the door, mentally preparing to endure an evening of playing by Gage's ever-changing rules, but my toiletry bag caught my eye. Had I left it out this morning? I must have because I'd been the last one in here.

Stupid. So stupid.

Holding my breath, I listened for footsteps. There were none. I wandered closer to the bag and dug through it until I found what I was looking for. The makeup compact felt cool and solid in my hands—a sharp contrast to the dread that burned in my gut. Before I questioned the wisdom of my actions, I pulled out the tiny piece of paper and unfolded it.

I'd found the note taped to the front door one day, shortly after Gage had ended my sentence in his cage, and things between us had gone back to a weird sort of normal. But if he found this…

I shuddered to think of the consequences.

The paper was worn around the edges from taking it out often and reading the simple two-word message, jotted down in a familiar heart-wrenching scrawl.

I'm okay.

4. SILENCED

"I thought you could help me with something next week," Gage said after dinner. As Eve splashed in the tub, I turned and found Gage's impressive form filling the open doorway. At first, I thought he was talking to her, as he often came up with things for her to do because she loved helping.

But he was talking to me. His blue eyes held that familiar sparkle that turned my insides to mush. Gage wore many faces—Master, sadist, disciplinarian, and right now, loving husband. He had something up his sleeve. Something I was going to be happy about. He stepped into the bathroom and sat at the edge of the tub.

"Channing Enterprises is sponsoring an event in a couple of weeks."

I raised a brow, wondering where he was going with this.

"Basically, it's an overpriced masquerade ball." He let a beat pass. "But a portion of the proceeds will go to The Eve Foundation."

Wow. Over the summer he'd formed The Eve Foundation to help fight childhood cancers, claiming it was something he'd been thinking about doing for months. But I suspected he'd done it because regardless of his questionable actions, he did have a conscience. Maybe he even felt a little guilty for demanding I stop volunteering at the hospital. I still had no life outside of motherhood or my marriage, but at least he was beginning to cut me some slack.

And I couldn't help but find a sliver of hope in the unexpected arrival of this conversation. Unable to stop myself, I leaned forward and pressed my lips to his.

He laughed. "Does that mean you'll help me with this?"

"I'd love to. What do you need me to do?"

"Each sponsor is helping with the organization of the event. I have a team working on theme and decor, but they might as well be color blind, so I fired them yesterday."

"Oh," I said, a touch of nervousness painting my utterance.

"I want elegant, classy, *and* seductive. What I don't want is a standard costume party." He lowered his voice, shifting his attention to Eve for a moment, but she was too busy building a humongous bubble castle in the tub to care about boring adult conversation. "You are the epitome of all three, and I know you can do this, even on such short notice."

His confidence in me heated my belly in a way that wasn't sexual for once. Sex drove our relationship to the extreme, which made these small moments of coexisting as husband and wife all the more special. "I'll do my best. I mean, I do know your tastes pretty well. I was your personal assistant once upon a time."

He raised a brow as if giving what I'd said consideration. "Good. Then it's settled. I'll clear my afternoon for you on Tuesday and Wednesday." With a smile, he leaned down and scooped up a bubble, then smeared it on Eve's nose. As she giggled and squealed, he took the opportunity to whisper in my ear. "But enough about work. After you tuck in Eve for the night, I want you downstairs on your knees. I laid something out for you."

My full ass was a reminder of what was to come, and the happy vibe of a moment ago dissipated. The fact that he was going to do this in the basement filled me with even more dread. I didn't know why the idea of anal terrified me so much. It wasn't like we hadn't done it before. In fact, he'd introduced anal sex within the first week of blackmailing me into being his.

But things had been different. Back then *everything* about him had terrified me, and I hadn't had a choice.

And you have a choice now?

In a way, I did. Or at least, I had. He'd given me a choice before I'd stupidly let go of my right to refuse on our anniversary. Now anal sex had become this huge *thing* between us—and an even bigger thing in my head— where I waited in dread for him to do it while he taunted me with the fact that he was going to fuck me that way.

And he always took his time, as if he lived to take me

in such a demeaning way, drawing out my discomfort and fear along with the mind-blowing orgasm at the end.

I finished bathing Eve and tucked her in for the night, then immediately wished I'd come up with an excuse to stall. Hovering outside her bedroom, I did my best to come up with something that needed to be done *now*.

There was nothing. I'd finished the nightly chores, and Eve was already snoring softly in that precious way she had about her. The only thing left was my avowed duty to my husband.

It was time to be his obedient slave.

I padded down the hall and spied Gage in his office. He sat at his desk, one hand propping up his head while his sharp gaze roamed the screen of his laptop. I should just head down to the basement and prepare. It's what he expected. What he wanted. But I couldn't bring myself to do it. Pushing the door open further, I glanced at the cage in the corner, now hidden behind the facade of a cabinet that locked. The black metal panel stared me in the face whenever I set foot inside his home office, a constant threat. I was one serious misstep away from finding myself back in there.

"Eve in bed?" he asked.

"Yes."

"Do you know how hard I am for you right now?" He didn't lift his head, and I wanted to go to him just to run my fingers through his thick, dark strands.

"No, Master," I said with a nervous swallow. "How hard?"

"Hard enough to break you in two. Don't make me

punish you for stalling."

Shit, shit, shit.

He had me wound so tightly I could hardly breathe. I hurried from his office and down the stairs of the basement. Something sat on the end of the bed, just like he'd promised, but it took me a full minute to find the courage to see what it was.

Thigh highs and a garter belt. No panties. That wasn't the distressing part. No, the O-Ring gag and nipple clamps had me pulling my hand back, as did the accompanying note.

Put them on, then wait for me on your knees.

Was I in trouble? But that didn't seem right. He was always the one to put the clamps on and shove the gags in. I couldn't imagine him giving the honor to me if I were about to receive a punishment.

But I hadn't misread the note. He wanted me to do it this time. God, Gage would not be happy until I surrendered every last piece of myself. He'd been slowly breaking me down from the moment he caught me stealing from him. Even after we'd married, he'd continued to play me like a well-loved guitar.

The Friday Night Ritual, which still occurred without fail. The sly introduction of all the things I'd "negotiated" against before we got married.

No bullwhip? Now used once a month to remind me of how I'd failed him with Ian.

No nipple clamps? Now used whenever he fucking felt like it.

As far as gags went, he didn't wait to catch me in a lie

anymore. He used them freely as well. Ever since I'd flirted with disaster all those months ago, he'd basically tossed my hard limits out the window, and he'd been pushing past them ever since.

Week after week with more severity. Pushing just a little...bit...*more.*

My guilt hadn't let me object at first. I'd felt he was justified in doing whatever he wanted, considering what I'd done. But then things had shifted, and we'd found our footing. He'd even returned my cell and the key to my car —albeit with restrictions.

But the hard limits...he kept bulldozing right over them as if they didn't exist.

And I kept surrendering, just as I was doing now, knowing that my ass was about to get fucked. I undressed, then rolled the stockings up my legs, stretched my lips around the gag that was big enough to accommodate his cock, and pinched my nipples tight between his clamps, making sure they hurt like hell because if I didn't, he'd make me regret it.

Unclipping my hair, I let the red locks fall to my shoulders as I dropped to my knees. Hands clasped at the small of my back, and breasts thrust out. I'd perfected this pose over the last year and a half, and he ate it up every time.

He made me wait longer than usual tonight— probably because he wanted me slightly unhinged. By the time his confident gait sounded on the stairs, my nipples were numb, my knees throbbed as much as my pussy did, and drool bathed my chin and chest. I didn't dare look at him. Suddenly, I was scared. This felt like...

Like a punishment.

He sauntered closer, bare feet coming into view, and pushed his eager hands into my hair—hair that had grown by a few inches since I'd whacked it off in anger. Gently, he tilted my chin up.

"I see the confusion in your eyes. You're wondering if you're in trouble." He knew me so well. As he ran his thumb over my lips, tracing the shape of my stretched mouth, I could do nothing but return his stare. "You're not in trouble *this time*, but I am disappointed in you."

I tried talking, despite the humongous gag making my jaw ache, but he pressed a finger to my tongue.

"I wanted you unable to speak for a reason. You're going to listen carefully, Kayla. There is *nothing* between Katherine and me, except for Conner."

He saw me earlier. Damn.

"I have never been unfaithful, baby. Not in the flesh, and certainly not in here," he said, pointing to where his heart beat. "I live and breathe to be your Master. To be your everything."

Couldn't he see that he was? I'd fought it like hell, but in the end, Gage was my everything. I'd given so much of myself to him.

"I only want to protect you. Things are about to get ugly between Katherine and me, and I don't want you caught in the crossfire. She can be downright vindictive when she doesn't get what she wants." He stepped back, lowering his fingers to the front of his unbuttoned slacks, and slowly pulled down the zipper. His cock sprang free, a hard piston already leaking at the tip. "She's not even close to getting me in her bed, and she knows it." He exhaled on a long sigh as he took his cock in his hand and slowly stroked the length from base to tip.

"This is all you, baby. The thought of your mouth on me, the way you submit even when you're scared, the fire you carry around inside of you. I've got a fucking cramp in my wrist from jacking off so much this week."

Crouching in front of me, he pinned me with an earnest gaze full of intensity. "She showed up at my hotel room. I won't lie to you and tell you she wasn't at the conference."

Of course she'd attended. He hadn't fired the bitch—he'd merely transferred her to another office after I'd thrown a fit about her working with him. My eyes must have grown huge with jealous rage. He sifted his fingers through my hair—a habit he'd picked up whenever he figured I needed calming.

"When are you going to learn that you have nothing to worry about?" he asked. "I slammed the door in her face, then I jacked off to thoughts of ramming my cock down your throat. I don't know how much more honest I can get than that."

Matching actions to words, he rose to his feet and shoved his cock through the opening in the gag. He was silky smooth on my tongue and big enough to fill the cavity of my mouth to the back of my throat.

"Ah, fuck, baby. You own me with that wicked mouth. You take my cock so well—better than any woman ever has." His gaze ignited a burn so deep that I felt it to my bones. Every atom in my body sizzled for him, existed solely for this man who had no qualms about turning me inside out.

"Why would I want anyone else when I've got you here on your knees, so fucking eager to please me?"

His words made me light-headed with a sense of power. I grabbed his hips and brought his shaft deeper until I had him moaning and thrusting in abandon.

"Trust me, baby," he said with a grunt. "You take my cock like you were born for it. Give me your sweet ass too." He grabbed my head between two steady hands and held me in place while he plundered.

He wasn't gentle.

He wasn't merciful.

He had my number, read my body language as if it had been written for him, and he wasn't about to let me steal a shred of power. Self-preservation kicked in, and I pushed against his hips. Useless. He gripped me tighter and rammed his cock more roughly down my throat.

I gagged so hard that my stomach cramped, and my knuckles whitened as my hold on his hips turned to one of desperation. My throat burned, and tears of frustration leaked from the corners of my eyes. I tried relaxing my throat to accommodate his thrusts, but my gag reflex seemed to be on steroids. I glanced up at him, silently seeking mercy, and found his eyes hazed over with domination.

"I own you. Own you, *own* you," he chanted with each plunge. "Fuck, Kayla..." Letting out a ragged groan, he withdrew from my mouth with a quick jerk. "Almost ended me."

Reserved, control-freak Gage was nowhere in sight. In his place was this lust-filled man who was slowly letting his walls crash right before my eyes. I wasn't sure how it was possible for two people to live in the same house, month after month, and never really know each other.

But we'd managed it. I hid parts of myself from him —like that forbidden note at the bottom of my bag which had given me the answer to a question I wasn't supposed to know. Wasn't *allowed* to know. But in this moment, our truest selves shone through, and the protective veil between us lifted. He had me on my knees with my ass plugged and nipples clamped as he fucked my mouth, yet he was as vulnerable as me.

My reaction to seeing him with Katherine had pulled at something inside him. He didn't like that I doubted him. And he had every reason to be upset because he'd never given me a reason to suspect he'd cheat.

But I couldn't say the same for myself. I'd not only given him a reason, but I *had* touched another man, and not just any man, but the one he despised most in the world.

"As much as I adore your mouth," he said, rolling the tip of his shaft against my tongue, "my cock is going in your ass. You can love it, or you can tolerate it. Either way, you're taking it." He pulled out, removed the gag, and hoisted me to my feet. "Get on the bed. I want you on your stomach with your knees tucked under you."

I obeyed his commands, my breathing as erratic as my heart beat. "Like this?"

"Almost. Raise your ass." He climbed behind me. "That's better. Reach behind you and spread your cheeks."

Silence followed his words. This was it. The ultimate surrender.

"Do it now, Kayla."

"Master…" My voice faltered, but my body knew its place before my brain did. I submitted to his orders, even though I found it humiliating. Fingers shaking, I spread my cheeks in invitation, leaving myself open and vulnerable. This was about trust. If I could offer myself while remaining completely still…truly submitting the one hole I didn't want to give…then he'd win this game tonight.

But maybe I would too because meeting the challenge of pleasing him fulfilled me in a way that most would view as sick and wrong. And maybe it was.

But it *felt* right.

Whether or not his cock felt right inside my tight hole was another story. He inched out the plug that had grown too dry, applied a liberal amount of lube, then held a palm in front of my mouth for good measure.

"Spit."

I spat saliva into his hand.

"Are you wet?" he asked.

"Yes, Master." Shamefully so.

"Good girl. Now beg your Master for a good ass-fucking."

The word *please* was on the tip of my tongue, just waiting to spill off my lips. That single word would give him exactly what he wanted, and in a roundabout way, it would give me what I wanted too.

But the journey was going to hurt like hell. No doubt about it.

"I'm waiting."

"Master...please." My voice sounded small and uncertain.

"Please, what? You're going to have to be more specific."

Gage was at the top of his game, and he wasn't about to back down. Splaying my ass cheeks wasn't enough—he intended to drag the words from my soul.

I cleared my throat and forced my pride down, but it sat in my gut like deadweight. "Please put your cock in my ass, Master."

"Sexiest fucking words I've ever heard." He eased inside me, just the tip at first, and stretched and pushed, gaining more of my ass with each inch forward. Fuck, it hurt. No denying that it did, and I could do nothing but lay there and try to relax, try to accept his girth because he was filling me no matter what.

And that was the most disturbing part of our relationship. Gage didn't need my consent because I'd given it the day I married him. He was in charge. *He* decided all things. Sure, I could change my mind. If I left him.

He knew I wouldn't. He made sure I wouldn't. Our marriage was unhealthy and distorted, but I didn't care anymore. Like a true addict, I kept coming back for more.

With a growl that bordered on possessive, he seated

his full length inside my tight space, and somehow, despite the pain and the fear that had grown too big in my head, taking his cock in my ass felt a little like him coming home.

5. THUMBED

Weekends were always busy, especially when Conner came to visit. The kids got along, for the most part, filling the house with their boisterous games and laughter.

Except for when they didn't.

I'd take rambunctious play any day over the bickering going on in the other room, escalating to a feverish pitch with each "stop it!" from Eve. This wasn't good, especially since Gage was trying to catch up on work so we'd have the day to spend with the kids.

Abandoning the pita pockets I was putting together for lunch, I hurried from the kitchen and spotted the two of them sitting side-by-side on the couch in the living room. Conner held a game controller in his hand, but he focused mostly on Eve. Every few seconds, he flicked the crayon she clutched in her fingers, making her draw a jagged line.

"Conner!" I said before Eve could screech in protest again. "Leave her alone. That isn't nice. I'm sure you wouldn't want her picking on you like that."

He sprang up from the couch, tossing the controller onto a cushion, and faced me with his arms crossed. "You're not my mom. I don't have to listen to you. My mom said so!"

Oh boy. I gaped at Conner for a couple of seconds, trying to come up with an effective response to get through to him, but his angry expression settled into one of apprehension. Conner's blue-eyed gaze darted past me, and I sensed Gage's presence before he spoke.

"Go to your room. *Now*."

"I hate it here!" Conner stomped toward the hallway in a grand ceremony of disapproval.

Gage sighed. "I'll talk to him." He squeezed my shoulder before following his son.

Helpless frustration burned my eyes. I should've handled the situation better. Unable to sit and do nothing, I told Eve to stay put before creeping down the hall toward Conner's bedroom. Gage had moved the gym equipment into the basement so Conner would have his own space when he visited…which wasn't as often as we'd like, considering Katherine fought Gage every step of the way. If she'd stop being a bitch for one second and do the right thing, maybe Conner wouldn't keep having these outbursts. The poor kid needed a little stability— not random weekend visits with a father he barely knew.

Gage's voice filtered through Conner's open doorway. I hesitated on the outskirts, not knowing if I should intrude or not. Better to stay put. Conner wouldn't likely open up with me there anyway.

"This is stupid. Why do I have to come here?"

"Because you're my son," Gage said, drawing in a deep breath. He softened his tone. "I know this is confusing for you. I know you miss your mom and Sean," he said, referring to Katherine's ex, who, for several years of Conner's life, had been the only father he'd known. But since Katherine's deceit had come to light, Sean had washed his hands of the boy who wasn't biologically his.

"I just wanna go home."

"This is also your home, and you have a family here that loves you too."

"They aren't my family."

"Yes, they are, and I won't put up with you disrespecting Kayla or Eve."

"My mom said they'd be gone soon." Conner's voice hitched. "It's supposed to be me, you, and my mom!"

Heavy silence followed his words, then Gage cleared his throat. "That isn't going to happen, Conner." Footsteps sounded, and Gage muttered for him to take a few moments to calm down before coming out to apologize for his behavior.

Gage halted in the hallway as soon as he caught me lingering outside of Conner's bedroom, his indigo gaze blazing with ire.

"You know how I feel about eavesdropping." Closing the distance between us with purposeful steps, he gently took me by the elbow and escorted me to our bedroom. The lock clicked into place, and he whirled to face me, arms crossed.

"I'd have you on your knees right now if we had time."

"I didn't do anything wrong." The instant the words left my lips, I wanted to yank them back. Okay, so eavesdropping wasn't exactly an innocent act to engage in, but it was a minor fuck-up. The problem with Gage was he punished all infractions, no matter how small.

"You know that's not true," he said, his tone calm and even. Moving around me, he sauntered to the chair he used to dole out spankings and settled into the soft leather. "Which is why you're going to come over here this instant and present your ass. I don't have time for you to stall." He patted his lap.

I blew out an exasperated breath, but I went to him without further prompting and draped over his thighs. He flipped my skirt up and exposed my bare bottom, and a hot tingle erupted between my legs as I waited for the first strike of his palm.

"You're getting wet, aren't you?"

I dropped my head with a groan. "I'm sorry, Master. I can't help it."

"I believe you. So here's what I'm going to do to help you refrain from becoming aroused. I'm going to use a different method of punishment."

Before I could ask about this "different method," he shoved his thumb into my tight hole. Abruptly, violently, and uncompromisingly.

"Ow! Master, please!" I hissed in a breath, clenching my ass around the dry intrusion of his thumb.

"Spanking is losing its effectiveness. Hell, even my belt turns you on, and a punishment should hurt. It should, at the very least, make you uncomfortable. Don't you agree?" Slowly, he withdrew his thumb and forced it back in again.

"Ow!" I shrieked.

"Answer me, Kayla."

"Yes, Master!" Ow, fuck *ow*! He wasn't using a drop of lube, and that made it hurt even more. "I'm sorry! Please, Master. I won't do it again."

"I don't imagine you will after this." The horrible burning eased up for a mere second as he removed his thumb, but relief was short-lived. He pushed it in once more, to the hilt, and stretched my burning anus in every direction.

"Please stop," I sobbed. He hadn't truly hurt me in months. He'd played with my backdoor, even fucked it a couple of times, and of course, he spanked me regularly. But he was correct in assuming spanking no longer worked as a punishment.

"I will not allow you to backtrack in your behavior," he said, keeping his thumb lodged in my ass. "The last time I gave you an inch, you took a hundred fucking miles and ended up in a compromising situation." He let a significant beat pass. "Or do you need to spend some time in the cage to remind you?"

"No! Please, no, Master."

"You know what is and isn't allowed. Eavesdropping has never been and will never be accepted. Do you understand me?"

"Yes, Master."

"I was in there scolding Conner for disrespecting you, only to find you doing the same to me. When I told you

I'd speak to him, you knew I meant alone. Did you not?"

"I did. I'm sorry I overstepped." I hesitated, wanting to say more but not sure if I should. Eventually, the need to be heard won. "I hate being left out. I feel like I'm the last to know about everything."

"Baby, I have no intention of leaving you out. I was going to discuss Conner's behavior with you later after I'd talked to him alone." Even though he softened his tone, he did not cease his assault on my ass. "If you want to know something, you need only to ask. Eavesdropping will not be tolerated."

Some tiny part of me acknowledged he was right about the eavesdropping. But the headstrong part of myself—the facet of my being he was most challenged by —called bullshit. Considering his growing fascination with all things anal, I knew he'd find excuse after excuse to use my ass for his sadistic pleasure by putting the stamp of punishment on it.

A girl, no matter how obedient and submissive, could only stay silent for so long. "Is this really a punishment, or is this just another way for you to get your rocks off?"

He laughed, the sound so rich and unexpected that I jumped. "Both, Kayla. You want to know if my cock is hard? Fuck yeah, it is, in case you hadn't noticed. If we didn't have two kids needing us in the other room right now, I'd fuck you senseless." He dug his thumb in a little more deeply, and I cried out another plea for him to stop.

Useless pleas because Gage operated by his own rulebook, and the word "stop" wasn't part of his repertoire.

"Hell, I'd fuck this ass senseless, and you'd let me, wouldn't you, baby?"

The hardwood floor blurred through the tears collecting in my eyes. They weren't tears of sorrow; they were pure drops of pain burning my eyeballs—a testament of my frustration.

"What if I said no?"

He laughed again. "You don't know how to say no to me. Let's talk about the fact that I have you willingly lying across my lap with my thumb up your ass. Does it hurt?"

"Yes!"

He added a sound wallop to my butt cheek in addition to his anal probing. "Address me properly."

"Yes, Master! It hurts."

"Does it turn you on?"

"No, Master." Not unless he added some lube and played with my clit—behavior he wasn't likely to engage in at the moment.

"Do you like it when I punish your little hole?"

"No, Master." What type of questions were these?

"Then all things considered, I'd say this is a very effective form of discipline. And it pleases me how willingly you accept it." With a final swat to my bottom, he removed his thumb and gently helped me off his lap.

Silently, I vowed to be on my best behavior because pleasing him not only made my life easier, but it caused my body to hum in a way I couldn't help but crave. I dropped to my knees and let my lips linger on his left bare foot, followed by his right.

"Thank you for your discipline, Master."

His eyes widened the slightest bit. He hadn't expected such a display of voluntary acceptance on my part. Truth be told, I hadn't either. But sometimes accepting my place was far better than fighting it. My reward lay in his eyes; a warm hue of appreciation.

"You're welcome. You can always count on my discipline. As for this particular kind of anal punishment, I plan to use it often. So remember that the next time you think of stepping out of line. Not only will I spank your ass, but I will punish your hole as well."

"I understand, Master." I didn't, but I understood it was what he wanted to hear, and the submissive in me delighted at his surprised reaction. Sometimes, a girl just had to keep her Master on his sexy toes. "May I finish fixing lunch now, Master?"

"You may. I'll get the kids ready."

I rose fluidly, aiming for graceful yet sexy, and moved to leave. At the last second, he pulled me onto his lap again, this time to sit.

"I forgot something," he said, voice raspy with sudden desire. His attention fell to my mouth, and in response, I parted my lips. Tangling a fist in my hair, he angled my head and claimed my lips with a ravenous mouth. His tongue pushed inside, battling my own, and we both moaned into the kiss.

Then he let me go as suddenly as he'd grabbed me. "*Now* you may finish making lunch."

6. ELEPHANTS

Conner was downright morose during lunch. But at least Eve had bounced back from our rocky morning.

"Then Leah said she liked Toby, but Toby and his stupid friends found out. The boys were so mean to her!" She glared at Conner. "I'll never like boys. Gross."

He glared right back, and that warning glint in his blue eyes sent a chill down my spine. He certainly had the best of Gage in him—his fierce loyalty, for one—but every now and again I glimpsed the same dominant curve to that boy's smile.

But Conner was far from smiling now. He hadn't said a word since we'd all sat down for lunch. To say he was unhappy at losing video game privileges was an understatement. Eve either didn't care, or she was oblivious. She continued her hundred-mile-per-hour chatter.

"I'm sooo glad Leah isn't a boy," she said. "Or we couldn't be friends." Eve scrunched her nose. "But she likes boys!" she said, rolling her eyes. "Why do girls like boys, Mom?" She'd stopped calling me "Mommy" at the start of first grade, because apparently, Leah said it was a baby thing to do.

"That's a good question." Why *did* we put up with men? We not only liked them, but we fucking loved them —even when they left our asses tender from obscene punishments. It was insanity.

"Is Simone still your best friend?" Eve asked me.

The girl had a sharp memory. Before I could answer, Gage interjected.

"Actually, your mom is spending the day with Simone on Monday."

I turned a stunned gaze on him. He shot me a grin, the tilt of his mouth hinting at how happy my submission earlier in the bedroom had made him.

"Your mom works hard around here to take care of us," he told Eve. "I think it's time she had a day to herself. What do you think, kids?"

"Can I go, too? Pleeease?" Eve whined.

"Sorry, princess. You've got school."

Conner shoved his plate away. "Can I be done? I wanna go to my room."

I thought Gage was going to object, but the dejected sigh he let out instead pricked at my heart. He was trying so hard to connect with Conner.

"Go ahead."

The legs of Conner's chair scraped the floor, and he left the room without ceremony. The boy spent most of the day in his room until Gage made him join us for a board game.

And that was how the weekend passed—uneventful and unbearably slow. Normally, it wouldn't bother me so much, but I had plans for the first time in months, set in stone later that night after Gage programmed Simone's number into my cell and gave me permission to call her. For whatever reason, he was giving me a reprieve from the monotony of my life for a day.

My fingers clutched my cell, but I didn't move to make the call. No, my first instinct was to question him on his unexpected generosity, but upon his eyebrow quirk, I shoved my reservations aside and dialed Simone.

Permission was permission. And hell, I was excited at the prospect of a girls' day out.

Regardless, I couldn't help but dissect the implications. Either aliens had taken over Gage's body, or punishing me in the ass had put him in a damn good mood. It was the only explanation I could come up with because Simone had been a sore spot in our recent history ever since she'd come to me about Ian's cancer. Not that Gage had cared for her to begin with, but this was the first time in...*ever* that he'd given me the go-ahead —on his prerogative, for that matter—without so much as a sideways glance.

And that made *me* the suspicious one. It made the stubborn part of my mind latch right onto Katherine again, agonizing over the what-ifs. By the time Monday arrived, I'd given in to the poisonous doubts plaguing me. I was in full-on paranoid mode.

Simone was unusually quiet from across the small table for two at our favorite bistro. Tilting my head, I tried catching her gaze. She'd barely said two words since we'd given the waitress our lunch orders. I knew she wasn't happy with the way I'd gone MIA for the last few months, but I'd naively thought we could pick up where we'd left off. I'd naively thought she'd understand. I should have known better.

"I'm kind of surprised you called," she said, breaking the silence.

"I'm sorry, Simone."

I didn't have a choice.

She'd disagree. Everyone had a choice, she'd say in that indignant tone of hers. The rational part of my brain —the part that wasn't led around by Gage's cock—would agree with her.

"That's all you're going to say after giving me radio silence for so long?"

The waitress arrived with our orders, which gave me a few moments to figure out how to go forward with this tricky conversation. Spilling my guts to her used to be easy, but now tension simmered between us, and I hated every second of it.

"You know I have certain…rules to follow. Things got complicated after…"

After Ian.

So much to discuss, but I couldn't even bring myself to say his name. She shifted, tilted her head, and I recognized the signs. Go on, she silently told me.

"After everything that happened, Gage and I had a lot of issues to work through." What a fucking understatement. She didn't know the half of it. She knew more than most people did about my fucked up arrangement with my husband, but I wasn't about to speak of those torturous months spent in his cage, bound and gagged for my sins. If I opened that can of *disturbingly wrong*, I'd have to justify his actions, and somehow, they only sounded justifiable in my poisoned mind. There was just no way of explaining that to her. "I didn't mean to shut you out, Simone."

She took in a breath, then blew it out, ruffling her blond hair. "I get it. You obviously have baggage you don't want to get into. I'm just glad you're finally back." Her brows furrowed over deep brown eyes. "You are back, right? No more disappearing on me for months at a time?"

A weak smile took hold of my lips. "I think things are starting to settle down again."

"So you worked shit out?"

I heard so much more in that question—all the ones she didn't ask. The ones she would probably never ask because she respected my boundaries too much to pry. Hell, she respected my boundaries better than my husband did.

"We're getting there," I hedged.

"I've got a nosy ear, you know." She fit her palm behind her right ear, and I had to laugh. But then the image of Gage and Katherine whirled through my head and blew that small amount of joy to the next county over.

"I'm scared he's fucking her." The words tore from my mouth before I could stop them. And damn, they weren't even true...entirely. I believed him when he said he wouldn't touch her...didn't I?

"Who?" Simone bit into her BLT sandwich.

"Katherine."

She halted her chewing long enough to raise a brow, then a few moments later, she wiped her mouth with a napkin. "She's still an issue?"

Hell, Katherine had been an issue since the day Gage had first hired me on as his personal assistant. She was the weed that refused to go away. Her presence just spread and spread until the bitch sprang up in the cracks of our marriage.

"I don't know. He swears nothing is going on with her."

"You think he's lying?"

"I..." I replayed his words in my mind, and deep down I knew he'd meant them. "No. Not really. But she just has a way of getting to me. She touches him every chance she gets, shows up at his hotel room—"

"She *what*?"

I nodded, feeling even more miserable. "He said he slammed the door in her face." I wondered what Simone's reaction would be if I told her the rest—how he'd jacked off while imagining his cock in my throat. I parted my lips and drew in a thready breath.

"It really boils down to one thing. Do you trust him?"

She made it sound so easy, but as I examined my feelings and tore apart his words, dissected his actions, I realized that I did. Mostly. There were plenty of things *not* to trust him about—anytime he came near me with his cock at the ready and a belt or whip in his fist, for instance—but on a fundamental level, I did trust him.

If I didn't, why would I keep putting myself through this? Why keep bending and bending and bending?

"I do trust him," I said, swiping my bangs to the side. "I love him. More than I could ever say. More than even makes sense."

"Then I'd put the baby mama out of your head. He married *you*, and though I won't begin to understand or approve of your…weird relationship, he has always come across as pretty fucking whipped."

I almost spluttered my tea all over the table at her words. Gage, whipped? But the more I thought about it, the more it clicked, because when you got down to the nitty-gritty, we had each other wrapped. "I guess you're right. I just wish I could get that woman out of my head. The way she touches him, and the way she glares at me… God, Simone, she makes me see red and green at the same time."

"You need a fucking hobby." Simone's mouth twisted into a scowl, but her gaze softened as she said it to take out some of the sting.

"A hobby?" I asked, absently picking at my half-eaten quiche. Apparently, the subject of Katherine made me lose my appetite. Or maybe it was the smell of overcooked cheese. I pushed the plate away, scrunching my nose. "Why do you say that?"

Simone made a scoffing sound, and I glanced up to find her reclined in her seat, arms crossed. "To hear you talk, it sounds like your whole life revolves around Gage and what he may or may not be doing with Katherine."

A hobby might not be a bad idea. Maybe I could start collecting trinkets, like dolphins or dragons.

Or elephants.

Definitely elephants. Lord knew I had plenty of those in my life. Gigantic ones that ate up too much space and sucked up all the air. One stood between Gage and me in the form of Katherine. But the biggest one sat smack in the middle of Simone and me.

This elephant's name was Ian, and he'd grown too secure in his comfy spot since that damn note had magically appeared on my door. But it was easier, *safer*, to focus on my marriage and the interloper named Katherine. The subject of Ian was too dangerous. Too painful.

Simone must have agreed because she didn't bring him up once. Not to tell me he was okay—the note had already done that—and certainly not to tell me whether or not she'd spoken to him or seen him.

And maybe it was better this way.

"If you're really worried about Katherine," Simone said, "then talk to Gage. Just be honest with him. Tell him how you're feeling."

She made it sound simple. If only it were that easy.

7. PETITION

The following day I met Gage in his office at Channing Enterprises to work on the charity ball project, but it wasn't until Wednesday when I finally found my lady balls to broach the subject of Katherine. Even then, it took me a good hour of perusing color schemes while situated firmly on his lap, distracted beyond belief by his depraved hands.

"So this is your final decision?" Gage asked, gesturing by way of a nod toward the various colors, fabric textures, and decorations splashed across the screen of his laptop. His fingers tapped a staccato beat on top of his desk.

"You said elegant and sexy."

He pressed a kiss to my neck, and I felt the curve of his smile. "Mmm, you most certainly are."

"Did you really need my help with this, or were you just looking for an excuse to have me on your lap for a few days?"

"I never need an excuse to have you on my lap, Kayla. For any reason."

Damn, he was turning me on.

"Truth is," he said, "I miss you here at the office. I wouldn't mind you coming back as my assistant if that's something you'd like to do."

I angled my head and shot a wide-eyed gaze at him. "Are you serious?"

"Absolutely."

"I'd love to." More than love to. I ached to fill the void that leaving the workforce had caused.

"Then consider it a done deal." He pressed his mouth to mine before focusing on our project again. "Besides, where would I be without you? You pulled this together in two days flat, fixing the blunders of the idiots I hired to do this job in the first place."

Two days seemed too long for the amount of work I'd done, but at least I'd finally whittled the color scheme down to burgundy, mahogany, and the accent color of gold. "I'm thinking creme china trimmed in gold, red masks with gold feathers for centerpieces—like those," I said, pausing to point at a picture, "and sable linens for the tables."

The visual made me think of sex and sin—just like that restaurant had the night he'd taken me there before our anniversary. Riding his cock in that private dining booth had been terrifying and exhilarating. I wasn't comfortable with public displays of indecency, but apparently, Gage had an exhibitionist streak in his blood. God, the surprises kept coming when it came to my husband.

Thing was, I was tired of being the last to know about

shit. Taking comfort in his assertion over the weekend that I need only to ask, I finally found the words and did just that. "Why was Katherine here last week?"

He stilled the casual tapping of his fingers. "Was that so hard?"

I narrowed my eyes. "What?"

"Asking about Katherine. Was it so difficult to come out and say what's on your mind?" His fingers resumed their tapping. "You've taken to eavesdropping lately, and I don't like it. You don't have to be afraid to come to me, baby. I'd rather know what's on your mind than assume and guess."

"I'm sorry."

"Don't be sorry. Just tell me what's on your mind."

"Why does she keep coming here?" My breath hitched. Lord knew I wanted an explanation, but now that one was forthcoming, I didn't know if I were ready.

"She's the mother of my child. I'm afraid we're not getting rid of her anytime soon."

"She's only using Conner as an excuse to see you, and you know it."

"I won't deny it."

His words tunneled deep, impacting the center of my being. "But you promised nothing is going—"

"Because nothing *is* going on." He took my right nipple between two punishing fingers. "Don't you trust me?"

"I...I want to," I whispered, barely able to form the words beyond my pounding heartbeat and the piercing ache in my nipple.

"Well that's great to hear, Kayla," he said, tone brimming with sarcasm, "because I've been trying so fucking hard to trust you again. I need you to do the same. Katherine is not a threat to you. I promise you that."

"But she wants you." The admission soured my tongue.

"Yes, she does, and being the bastard that I am, I can't help but throw my hot-as-fuck wife in her face every chance I get. Does that explanation make you happy?"

Oh, yeah. More than it should. But it did nothing to alleviate the doubt in my heart. Gage might not be fucking her now, but what if he changed his mind someday? What if, years later, he grew bored with me?

"You said I was playing with fire with—"

"Don't you dare say his name." He practically growled the words, his voice beyond harsh, and his grip on me even harsher. "I will beat your ass red if you say his name."

"How is that fair? Katherine is like a fucking leech that won't let go, and you keep encouraging her. You're playing with fire, just like I was."

"I'm not interested in sleeping with Katherine, and I'm sure as fuck not in love with her. That's the difference."

I felt my face heat with humiliation and regret. How could I respond to that? I couldn't.

"I look at that cage every night," he said, "and I *yearn* to lock you in there forever. Then I'd know you're mine."

"But I am yours. Can't you see that?"

"Prove it to me."

"How?" I asked, voice rising in disbelief. What more could I possibly do to prove it to him?

"The night of the ball. It just happens to be a Friday, and I have special plans for you afterward."

"But…" I trailed off, confused. "I take your punishment every Friday without complaint. What more do you want from me?"

"Everything, Kayla. I want everything." He gestured to the color schemes on the screen, his index finger hovering over a photo of a jeweled mask in burgundy. "I told you about the charity ball, but I didn't tell you about our plans afterward." Grabbing my hair, he tilted my head back and placed his warm lips on my neck. "After the masqueraders leave and it's just a handful of Portland's most wealthiest deviants, I want you to submit *everything* to me. No ands, ifs, buts, or whys. I say spread your legs, and you ask, 'How wide, Master?'"

A lump formed in my throat—a mass of sickening fear. "You want to fuck me in front of other people?"

"I want you to submit in front of other people."

"I don't know if I—"

"I don't care about your feelings on this. You will do as I say." He pushed me from his lap. "Because you always do what I say." His gaze lowered to his hard-on. "Get on your knees and suck me off."

Yielding to his command, I knelt between his legs. His desk hid most of my body, but he pushed back a few inches to give me more room. Shoving the masquerade ball and what would come after from my mind, I had him unbuckled, unzipped, and his cock in my mouth in about five seconds flat.

He pushed his hands into my hair and gripped the strands, holding me to his lap with suffocating force.

"I guess now would be a good time to tell you that Katherine will be here any minute."

The movement of my eager tongue stalled around his shaft, and I tried pulling away, but he wouldn't let me. With a groan, he forced his cock deeper. "Take it all, baby. I want her to see how fucking unglued your mouth makes me. I want her to see this, Kayla. Let's give her a show she won't forget."

This plan of his excited me too much, and I gagged extra hard. He wound my hair around his fist and drew my lips up and down his velvety cock. As my lips closed around the tip, I raised my eyes to his, entranced by the startling blue depth of his need for me.

"God, you're sexy," he breathed.

A quick rap sounded an instant before a door creaked open then closed. Feminine footsteps crossed the room. Over the ruckus of heels, I detected the soft groan that escaped Gage's tight lips.

"I'm glad you called," Katherine's said in her grating voice, "though I would have met you someplace more private. Your office isn't my idea of—"

"As you can see," he said with a grunt, responding to the way I worked the underside of his cock, "I don't care about privacy. I get what I want, where I want, and when I want. And right now I want my wife's very talented mouth wrapped around my cock while I give you these."

The sound of rustling papers drifted to where I knelt on the floor, and as he slid them across the desk, he leaned forward, thrusting deeper.

Silence ensued for a few heavy seconds. "What is this?"

"A petition for parenting time."

I imagined Katherine's beet-red face and envisioned steam coming out of her ears.

"We were working out visitation just fine. You don't need to do this!"

"If you mean you used our son as a bargaining chip, then yes, I do imagine the status quo was working in your favor."

"Gage!"

"Do not fuck with me, Katherine. You won't like the outcome." Voice stringent with a warning, he fisted my hair even tighter, and I felt his thighs quake under my clenched hands. He was losing his shit, though it was a toss up if his crumbling composure was a result of his argument with Katherine, or from the way I swirled my tongue around the head of his cock. I studied his face and found a mixture of both.

"I'll see you in court." A telling tick hardened his jaw an instant before he showed his teeth. "Now get out of my office so I can properly fuck my wife."

An indignant huff sounded, followed by stomps and a slam of the door. Gage yanked me to my feet, lifted me with one arm as he shoved the laptop out of our way with the other, and we crashed onto his desk. I wrapped my legs around him, my skirt bunching around my waist.

"Wish you could have seen her face," he said as he thrust into me with unapologetic violence. My body slid across his desk from sheer force. He crushed his lips to mine and devoured, our tongues tangling as he slammed my hands to the surface of his workspace. Clamping a hand around my wrists, he pinned them above my head as he plundered me into oblivion.

Fucked me to Neverland.

Loved me with more passion and obsession and loyalty than I deserved.

This crazy, obscene, and powerful man loved me. He hungered for me so much that he was about to rattle the screws loose that held his desk in one piece. He was definitely rattling the screws loose that held my mind together. With each thrust of his cock, they shifted a little more, slowly working their way out of the holes in my head. This was how my will shattered, how my sanity and the very essence of who I was broke into pieces.

Then he'd take those pieces and play with them as if they belonged to his favorite puzzle—one custom made for him. Maybe I was. Maybe I was born to be broken down and put back together by him.

"Fuck, baby," he said, pulling his mouth from mine. "If you believe nothing else, believe how much I belong to you. Feel me, Kayla." He slowed to a crawl, his cock annihilating me with measured strokes meant to push me right to the edge.

"The energy between us doesn't lie. It's more than fucking. It's mutual ownership. You have my heart. You *are* my heart."

Tears flooded my eyes, and a sob strangled from my well-kissed lips. My pussy clenched once around him, begging to go over the edge. Begging, always begging.

"I love you, Master."

"Ah fuck." He let go of my hands and engulfed me in an embrace rife with possessive restraint. "I love you so damn much." He huffed ragged breaths against my ear. "Come for me. Come so fucking hard the entire building hears it. Do it, baby."

When he was this worked up, holding back was impossible. I clenched around the steel-like shaft of my husband and cried his name at a decibel I was sure even Katherine heard.

"God, you feel good. So fucking good, squeezing my cock like you own it." His fingers grasped my hair and pulled.

I let out a high-pitched mewl, instantly forgetting where I was. In fact, I was pretty sure I forgot my own name. "Master," I cried, tears wetting my cheeks. "I need you…need you so much—ahhh! Don't stop! Oh God! Not yet."

I thought I'd plummeted off the cliff already, but I'd merely been floating, weightless in my desire for him. That first orgasm had been extraordinary, but this…I had no words, and no mind left to keep my wits about me. My cries escalated to a pitch that was ear-splitting. He shoved a sweaty palm over my mouth.

"They've heard enough. This is only for me." He swiveled his hips, his shaft rubbing in a way that slowly marched me to my end. I was going to tear myself apart in his arms. We fucked all the time, so why this time was so different, I didn't know. More emotions were involved, more *feeling*, more…everything.

"There, baby. You're *right* there, aren't you?" His lips curved into a sly grin. "But you're not coming again."

"Why?" I whimpered into his palm, eyes wide with a plea for mercy. Why was he doing this to me now? There was no way I could hold back, and the way he moved inside me told me he knew it. No, that sparkle in his indigo eyes spelled it out.

"Because I said so. But what I say doesn't matter right now, does it? You love my cock so much you're gonna cream all over it anyway."

I squirmed underneath his powerful body, spewing muffled protests into his sweaty palm.

"You don't have my permission." He closed his eyes for a moment and let out a harsh breath, then he removed his hand from my mouth.

Our bodies moved together like a well-oiled machine. We were meant to interlock in exquisite harmony, in rapturous agony. He was born to own, and I was designed to bend to his iron will.

"Please, Master," I whined. "Please let me come again."

"What will I get in return?"

"Anything you want."

"Be careful what you promise," he groaned. "I'll always hold you to your word."

Oh, he was sadistic as hell. I had no weapon to fight him, nor the strength. He plunged me to the heights of another orgasm—one that would cost me greatly—and as I contracted around his cock, I didn't miss that familiar devil's smile.

8. COUP

My time spent in Gage's office this afternoon had left me fucked on an emotional level. But it also shot me to a high from which I never wanted to come down. However, as soon as I pulled into my driveway and spotted Katherine's shiny red car sitting in Gage's parking spot, my mood plummeted so fast it could have caused whiplash.

She alighted from her vehicle with grating nonchalance as I shut off the ignition. Her arms, enhanced by subtle muscles that some men found sexy, crossed over the white bosom of her suit. I hated how she managed to embody the definition of *put-together*. Her red lips matched her nails to perfection, and hell...I wasn't blind. She'd look perfect and gorgeous on Gage's arm—another observation that gutted me.

Shoving aside my petty, envious thoughts, I headed to the front door, muttering a "what do you want?" on the way.

"Don't be nasty, Kayla. I'm only here to talk, woman

to woman."

I unlocked the door before turning to confront her toxic presence. "We have nothing to talk about." Shooting her a fake smile, I added, "So why don't you take your jealous ass home and go cry into a pint of Ben & Jerry's?"

Much to my irritation, she didn't seem affected by the barb. Casually, she glanced at her diamond-studded watch. "In about an hour, the only thing I'll be gorging on is your husband's cock." Her icy blue eyes widened, feigning incredulity. "You didn't think you were the only one sampling that fine cock, did you?"

"Get the fuck off of my property," I seethed.

She tsked-tsked. "You're just the trophy wife, Kayla. So that makes this *his* property. I'll leave when I'm ready."

I folded my arms and prayed for composure because I was two seconds away from tearing into her flawlessly made-up mug. I thought of Eve, and how she needed her mother at home instead of in jail.

Katherine pursed her painted lips. "Don't get me wrong. I'm sure Gage enjoys having you cook and clean and cater to his cock at his beck and call, but I've got a child to think about too. So I'm here to give it to you straight. Gage is in love with me. He's been fucking *me* for months, ever since he found out about Conner." For a fraction of a second, she had the nerve to appear contrite. "It's really not fair to you, or to me, so I think it's past time you know."

Clinging to my outward front of stoicism, I remained silent. But a porno of epic proportions flashed through my mind, starring Katherine and my husband, and I found my pretense in jeopardy of crumbling at any second.

Don't lose your shit now.

"You don't believe me, do you?"

"I trust my husband." Even as I said the words, I couldn't ignore the ever-present niggle of doubt. Forget the hypothetical porno. The memory of Katherine on her knees crashed into me with the violence of a hurricane. I ached to wash the recollection in red, ached even more to tear into the bitch and scratch the smugness from her face, blast the haughtiness from the curve of her pouty mouth.

I wanted her blood on my hands. I'd spatter every last piece of clothing Gage owned with crimson if he were fucking her.

Combing a manicured hand through her blond curls, she sauntered toward her car. The click-clack of her heels was akin to nails on a chalkboard.

"We both know there's no love lost between us, but you need to know the truth. I'm the mother of his child, and I refuse to be the mistress. Since he doesn't have the balls to tell you, then you need to come see for yourself."

She was lying. She had to be. Gage wouldn't...he *wouldn't.* If there was one thing I knew about Gage Channing, it was that I was the center of his universe.

Then why did she look so...triumphant?

I shook my head, refusing to buy into her lies. But as she pulled her car door open, lifting a shoulder as if to say, "Fine, don't say I didn't warn you," my lips parted and betrayed me.

"Where?"

She walked to my car and set a keycard on the hood. "The Hilton," she said, then rattled off a room number.

I waited until she slid into her driver's seat and backed out of the driveway before snatching the keycard from my hood. And as her luxury sedan disappeared down the road, I chewed over the decision ahead. I had three options.

Option A: Call Gage.

Option B: Ignore what Katherine had said.

Option C: Walk into that hotel room in an hour and see for myself.

The first option was not only the smartest, but it was the only option that would keep me out of trouble. The second was the most maddening, and the third was the one my unwavering doubt would demand I go with, to hell with the consequences. If checking this out for myself and finding that she was lying—that my husband was *not* cheating—would land me in hot water with Gage, then I'd accept the consequences. At least then, I'd finally be able to put these doubts to rest.

An hour later, I found myself creeping toward the door of an upper-floor room of the Hilton. Whatever lay beyond, I would accept and deal with it. But if what Katherine claimed were true...

Could I find the strength to forgive him? I wasn't sure, and that drove home how difficult it must have been for him to forgive my betrayal. I loved him so much at that moment, needed him more than I ever had because we'd both made mistakes, yet somehow we still formed a united front.

At least, I fucking hoped we did.

Sucking in a fortifying breath, I swiped the card and slowly pushed the door open. Nervous energy tingled down my spine as I crossed the threshold. With each step forward, my heels moving silently over the light textured carpet, I felt as if I were stepping into a bear trap, metal claws just waiting to rip into flesh.

Because if Gage were having an affair in this suite, wouldn't I hear something? And this hotel...it wasn't his style. Clearly, the room was a corner suite, outfitted with plush furniture that complimented the neutral theme of the space. Straight ahead, I spied two sitting chairs, but both were empty.

The place was nice, though nowhere near Gage's high standards. If he were going to cheat, I'd expect him to fuck me over in the Presidential suite of a place like the Heathman, at the very least.

I cleared the wall partitioning the vanity and bath area from the rest of the suite and found the king bed empty as well. The white comforter hadn't been disturbed, and the drapes were wide open, affording a view of the neighboring skyscrapers of downtown Portland.

What kind of sick game was Katherine playing? I reached for my cell. Calling Gage would mean he'd find out how I'd doubted him, and that would mean a harsh punishment on top of his hurt and disappointment, but I needed answers—answers only he could provide at this point.

A beep sounded, and the quiet swish of the door

reached my ears, followed by the soft pad of feet. I put my phone away and watched with a mixture of curiosity and apprehension. The last person I expected to see was Ian.

Apparently, he felt the same way. We both froze, eyes wide as we took each other in. I opened my mouth, trying to find a string of words that would make sense, but could find none. My mind raced ahead, mentally cataloging every detail of him—the healthy tint of his face and the subtle weight he'd put on since the last time I saw him.

Without thinking, I launched myself at him, overcome by too many emotions to name, and just held on to him. Tears dripped from my eyes, running in rivulets down my cheeks before soaking his black shirt.

"I'm sorry," I said with a sniffle. "I'm just so glad to see that you're okay."

He stepped back and tilted my head up with a gentle finger underneath my chin. "Hey, don't cry. I'm fine."

Nodding, I wiped my eyes, and the precarious predicament I now found myself in hit me hard. I stumbled toward the bed, only stopping when my legs gave out, and I sank onto the end in a stupor.

"But I am confused as to why you're here," he said as he claimed a spot on the other side of the mattress, being sure to keep plenty of distance between us.

"Umm," I blinked several times, running my fingers over the down comforter. "Katherine told me she and Gage..." Humiliation burned my cheeks, and I felt utterly ridiculous for believing her, for falling for her lies. I let out a long sigh that blew my bangs out of my eyes. "God, I was so stupid to believe her."

"You're not the only gullible one," he said. "I got a message that Gage wanted to meet with me, accompanied by this." He held up an identical key card.

"Bitch set us up," I muttered.

"Why would she do that?"

"Because she wants Gage, and…"

"And?" Ian prompted.

Oh, God. Panic fisted my heart, and all I could see was my husband's cock just mere inches from her lips. And Gage's threat that if I touched another man again…I covered my mouth, suddenly feeling sick. Upchucking would accomplish nothing, besides more embarrassment. I pushed down the burn of vomit in my throat and dropped my hand.

"I can't talk about it, so please don't ask." How could I be so fucking stupid? But damn, I still couldn't bring myself to regret that hug. Not one bit. Because the last time I'd laid eyes on Ian Kaplan, I'd been certain his death was imminent. But here he was, alive and healthy and…ironically all because the brother who hated his guts had found a morsel of mercy in his sadistic blood.

"Last thing I want is to cause you trouble," Ian said. "After the way I behaved earlier this year…."

"This isn't your fault. This is Katherine's doing, and I'll explain that to Gage." Never mind that he would be furious. I eyed Ian. Now that he was here, I could finally get some answers. "He told me what he did for you."

"Did he tell you his terms as well?"

65

Averting my gaze, I nodded. "You're not supposed to be here."

His mouth flattened into a stubborn line. "I know that's what he wants, but I can't live my life with our history hanging over my head forever. Don't you think it's time we put this behind us?"

"Of course I do! But Gage would rather burn in hell first. He's not going to budge."

"Well, getting a second chance at life has made me see things in a new light, Kayla. I have no control over what he does, or how he treats you." His hazel eyes, overflowing with the familiar kind of warmth I ached to wrap myself in, held me captive. "You're a strong, capable woman, so when you say you love him, I'm going to take you at your word." A beat passed. "I'm going to believe that you know what you're doing and can protect yourself."

"What are you trying to say?"

"I'm not leaving Portland, and I'm sorry if that's going to cause you problems." He shuttered his eyes for a moment. "I'm sorry if my decision to come back gets you hurt. But I've gotta live my life. I've accepted a job here, and…"

I raised my brows. "And?"

"And I'm seeing someone."

"Simone?"

He cocked his head in surprise. "How did you know?"

"Just a hunch."

And it was at that precise moment, as we were finally

on the cusp of putting all of our cards on the table, of burying past hurts and broken dreams, that another beep rang through the hotel room. A hint of footsteps kept me in suspense, breath stalling in my lungs. Terror tore through me, and my back stiffened, as my first thought was that Katherine had sent Gage.

But those footsteps weren't confident like my husband's. He had a unique way of walking, in which every step touched the ground with complete ownership of the path he chose to walk. These footfalls were dainty, completely feminine. When Katherine came into view, I shouldn't have been surprised. Of course she'd want to witness the coup she'd pulled off single-handedly.

However, I was even less prepared for the camera flash that went off in our faces.

9. SICK DAY

For the next two days, I stewed over one question: when would Katherine drop her bomb? Confessing to Gage was inevitable, but anytime I came close to opening up to him about what I'd unwittingly stepped into, my throat closed up on me.

I couldn't eat, couldn't sleep. Hell, I was so twisted up over Katherine's trickery—and her ultimatum that I leave Gage or she'd show him the photo—that I'd puked twice in 24 hours. At first, I thought it was due to stress, but then Eve came down with a stomach bug, so I blamed my sickness on a virus. Katherine and her nasty ultimatum faded into the background, as taking care of Eve trumped everything.

The scent of vomit seemed to cling to my skin. My poor baby hadn't been able to keep anything down for the past two hours since I'd picked her up from school. At least the worst had passed. I smoothed a palm over her hair while she snuggled into her princess themed sheets, lashes lowering from exhaustion. Gage would be home soon, so that didn't give me much time to shower.

Ten minutes later, as I towel-dried my hair, I heard his car pull into the driveway. I dropped the towel in the laundry hamper, ignoring how it hung over the side, and moved down the hall in time to greet him in the foyer.

"How's Eve doing?" Gage had barely stepped through the front entrance, smelling of autumn and pure sexy man, before he set his laptop case by the door, which was so unlike him. "I came as soon as I could. Where is she?"

"In bed." I hastened to keep up with his urgent stride as he headed down the hall toward Eve's bedroom. Finding her fast asleep, he stalled in the open doorway and let out a breath. I placed a hand on his back, touched by his concern.

"She's feeling much better. You didn't have to rush home from work."

He whirled, grabbed my arm, and pulled me a couple of feet down the hall. "Of course I did. You said she had a fever. She was puking…" Pacing a few steps, he pushed his hands into his hair.

"It's just a stomach bug. There's a lot of nasty stuff going around right now." I lowered my voice. "Really, Gage. I talked to her doctor. She doesn't think there's any reason to worry."

He turned to face me again, and something dark haunted his eyes. "How can you be so calm? So fucking sure? What if she's…?"

Sick again.

I swallowed hard to keep hysteria from choking me.

The fear that she would get sick again bordered on paranoia, and it would pull me into weeks, or even months of despair if I let it. I crossed the few feet separating us and wound my arms around him.

"I spent a whole year in Texas, in and out of the hospital. Every cough, every fever…I was a basket case convinced she was going to come out of remission."

"I hate that you had to go through that alone." Gage practically crushed me in his arms. "You're not alone now. Never again, baby."

Blinking back tears, I held on a little tighter. Eve coming down with any illness, no matter how common or normal, would always send me spiraling, and that was why I'd slowly learned to cope instead of freak out.

"She'll be fine," I said. "Remember the last time she got a cold? You went all protective daddy on her then too."

Which made me love him a million times more.

Exhaling on a sigh, he let me go. "Okay, I'll try to scale down the overprotective parent role. But Kayla…I can't help it. She's our girl."

I wanted to launch myself at him again, only this time with no clothing barring us from becoming a tangle of two bodies made for each other. I reached for his face, figuring I could settle for a kiss, but the hallway seemed to tilt. I shuffled backward until my spine hit the wall.

Gage frowned. "What's wrong?"

"I don't know. I'm a little dizzy."

"Did you eat lunch?"

"Umm…not that I can remember." I'd been too

worried about Eve to eat, and too busy taking care of her to find time to have lunch anyway. At the thought of food, my stomach revolted. What little I had eaten earlier that day rose so unexpectedly that making it to the bathroom wasn't a possibility. I tipped forward and vomited in the hallway, narrowly missing Gage's shiny black dress shoes.

He helped me to the bathroom and held back my hair as I lost more of my stomach's meager contents. "I'm sorry," I gasped during a spell. "Guess Eve's not the only one—"

My whole body seized, muscles tensing as vomiting turned to dry-heaving. "Oh God," I moaned. The dry-heaves lasted for maybe a minute, but it felt like forever. I fell back into Gage's arms, utterly spent.

"I happen to know a bed with your name on it," he said, carrying me as if I weighed nothing. Though his tone was light, he couldn't hide the worry in his eyes as he tucked me between our silky sheets.

"Thank you, Master."

Brushing the damp hair back from my head, he frowned. "Don't 'Master' me now, Kayla. Just rest. I'll keep an eye on Eve."

My eyelids suddenly felt as if they weighed a ton, but the fact that I was sick too was a huge relief. "See," I mumbled, halfway to a much-needed slumber. "She's fine. It's just a bug."

"Hopefully a short-lived one."

"Tonight's Friday, after all," I said. Now would be the time to tell him about my accidental meeting with Ian.

Then I could wash away my guilt over doubting Gage with the force of his punishing arm. But I didn't have any strength left, and I'd already spilled my guts enough for one day. I tried to muster a small smile, uneasy with the dark cloud hanging over my head. "Wouldn't want a pesky illness to get between your belt and my ass."

"You mean bullwhip," he said.

"It's been a month already?"

The sculpted shape of his jaw hardened. Hell, he was so damn beautiful. "It's been a month," he confirmed. "But I'm not about to use the bullwhip on you while you're sick, so we'll put an extension on it."

"An extension with interest?"

"We're discussing an ass-whipping, Kayla." He rolled his eyes. "Not negotiating a complex contract."

He was the king of complexity. Everything he did was calculated to break down another layer of my protective armor. A few hours later, after Eve and I sipped chicken broth and managed to keep it down, I sat in bed flipping through a fashion magazine.

Gage tucked Eve in for the night before returning to our bedroom. "You seem to be feeling better."

"I am," I said, putting aside the magazine as he settled onto the edge of the mattress.

His dark brows furrowed over indigo blue. "Could you possibly be…pregnant?" A note of hope colored his voice, ripping my heart to shreds.

"I don't think so." A small part of me wanted to hope too, but…

No.

Not worth the agony. Besides, I'd had a period a couple of weeks ago. "It was just the stomach flu." My shoulders slumped. "What if…?"

He took my hand and folded our fingers together. "What is it?"

"What if it's not in the cards for us?"

"I will not allow you to give up hope. Someday, I'm going to watch my child grow inside your gorgeous body. Have some faith, baby."

Faith didn't come easy. Deep down, I knew I'd disappoint him, and in more ways than one. Not only would I fail to conceive his child, but delaying my confession about Ian's return would crush him.

Crush him and make him irate enough to go off the rails.

10. CANDID CAMERA

By Saturday afternoon, Eve had fully recovered and was back to her rambunctious self, so we let her spend the night with Leah. Since we were kid-free for an evening, Gage took me out and wined and dined me.

"You're unusually quiet tonight," he said, taking a sip of his red wine. "Are you feeling under the weather again?"

"No, I'm fine." I gave him a small smile, but I felt sick as I forced a bite of steak down my throat. The need to spill my guts was eating me alive.

My reprieve from the Friday Night Ritual wouldn't last much longer. After we returned home from dinner, he would take the bullwhip to my ass. Time was running out. I had to find the courage to tell him about Katherine's trickery because I'd rather withstand a brutal punishment all at once and get it over with than suffer through his ritual, only to be punished again once he found out.

And he would find out. Katherine hadn't gone to all

of that trouble for nothing. She would send that photo to Gage eventually. My only advantage was coming clean before she did.

"You don't look fine. You seem upset."

A nervous breath escaped my mouth. "I did something you're not going to like." What an understatement.

He paused, fork dangling halfway to his mouth, and darkness shadowed his features for a moment. But then he quickly washed his face of it. "Finish your dinner, Kayla. Whatever it is, you can tell me when we get home."

"Okay," I said, relief choking that single word. There was no going back. Now that he knew there was something to tell, he would pry it out of me. I no longer had to agonize over how and when—it was in his hands now.

The rest of our meal slid down my throat, mostly tasteless. As for the wine, I'd barely taken two sips, knowing I'd need a clear head to handle what was to come. We left the restaurant, and he escorted me to the car with one hand pressed gently to the small of my back.

Heavy silence overshadowed the drive home, and the quick twenty-minute jaunt from the restaurant seemed much longer. Halfway through, Gage took my hand in his and offered his support. It was a simple gesture meant to reassure me that I could come to him about anything. But even as his fingers entwined with mine, I couldn't help but notice the anxious downturn of his mouth, and the way he steered the car single-handedly, his knuckles turning whiter with every mile.

As soon as we pulled into the driveway, Gage let go of my hand, and I missed the warmth of his touch instantly. He rounded the hood and opened my door—ever the gentlemen despite the brutality of his dominance. The wind rushed through the trees, scattering autumn leaves in a whirl. As we approached the front door, a cold drop of rain fell onto my nose.

"Just tell me one thing," he said, ushering me into the foyer. "Were you unfaithful?" His voice shook with nervous anger. But his eyes…fear had taken over, leaving him open and defenseless. It was such a foreign look on Gage that I did a double-take to make sure I wasn't hallucinating.

I wasn't. My dominant husband was terrified of what I might say.

Unable to help myself, I fit my palm against his cheek. Not touching him was impossible. "I haven't been unfaithful. I promise."

"Address me properly, Kayla." Warning tinged his tone. Now was not the time to fuck up on protocol.

"I'm sorry, Master." I sank to my knees, then dipped even further to kiss his shoes. "I wasn't unfaithful," I repeated.

Never again would I cheat on him, but he obviously still had reservations, or he wouldn't have brought it up the instant we crossed the threshold. Lifting my chin, I saw some of the worry fade from his gorgeous eyes.

He held out a hand. "Come on," he said, hauling me to my feet. After he removed my cashmere sweater and shed his overcoat, he ordered me to prepare for him in the basement. I'd known that was where I'd end up tonight, but a chill still tingled down my spine.

"Yes, Master." As I moved in the direction of his dungeon, limbs weak, I spied him pulling at his tie from the corner of my eye. Because he was eager to dress down to punish me? Or because the tension spiraling between us was choking him? I unlocked the door to the basement, switched on the light, and descended the stairs, chewing over his reaction the whole way.

I was Gage's only real weakness—something I failed to remember between the rituals and rigid expectations. He'd imprinted his power and mastery onto my soul, and I often forgot that underneath the confident veneer of dominance and control lived a vulnerable man with family issues.

And ex-girlfriend issues.

How could I prove to him that I wasn't going anywhere?

As I unzipped my dress and let it slide to the floor, the answer to that question tormented me. The only way to prove my loyalty was on my knees, unwavering in my surrender to his disciplinary decisions, no matter how intense the degradation and pain. I unclasped my bra, stepped outside the puddle of Haute Couture at my feet, and kneeled, preparing to speak Gage's language in the form of "yes, Master."

About fifteen minutes later, the door creaked open, and his loud footfalls brought him down the stairs. He walked with heavy feet as if the next hour or two weighed on his shoulders as heavily as they did mine. A single glance at his expression—eyes narrowed, jaw tense, and a pasty hue to his skin—and I knew I was too late. Katherine had gotten to him. As if to confirm my suspicion, he tossed a photo onto the floor in front of me.

"That just hit my inbox." He gestured to the incriminating evidence. "Is this what you need to tell me about?"

A glossy photo stared me in the face. Though Ian and I sat with plenty of space between us, our identical caught-in-the-headlights expressions made us look guilty. So did the fact that we were sitting on a bed in a hotel room.

"I can explain, Master."

"Can you, now?" He arched a contemptuous brow. "You said you weren't unfaithful. But Kayla," he said, crouching to confront me at eye level. "As far as I'm concerned, you cheated the instant you had any form of contact with him."

"It wasn't intentional, Master." God, I despised how tiny my voice sounded. How wobbly and terrified. The disconcerting part was the *why* of my fear. I wasn't afraid of getting punished—that was inevitable, and I'd accept it. No, what had my gut turning was his reaction to that picture. He wasn't only angry, but his entire body exuded betrayal, from the strain of his voice to the devastation in his eyes whenever his attention fell on the image of me with his brother.

"Wasn't *intentional?*" he said, rising to his full height. "Let me guess—someone kidnapped you and dropped you on that fucking bed with him. How convenient."

"I went there looking for you!" I squeezed my eyes shut, horrified at losing my cool. Raising my voice to my Master was never tolerated, a fact that was abundantly clear when I lifted my lids and found Gage rifling through the drawer where he kept my least favorite things. He strode toward me with a ball gag clutched in his hand. His breaths heaved in and out, and his massive chest expanded with every draw of air.

"Explain yourself." He dangled the humongous gag in front of my trembling lips.

Suddenly, I didn't want to explain. Recounting Katherine's unwelcome visit and how I'd fallen for her bullshit...no, how I'd doubted *him*...was almost more than I could stand.

"You're only making this harder on yourself," he warned.

The need to stall rose inside me, and I did my best to squash it. Submit. *Submit, submit, submit.* I chanted the word but finding the right way to explain how I'd essentially let my doubt tear a gaping hole into the fabric of our trust...that was easier in theory.

He exhaled on an exasperated sigh. "You've got sixty seconds before you lose the privilege of speaking."

His threat busted through my resistance. "After I left your office on Wednesday, Katherine was waiting for me in the driveway." The lies the bitch had spewed seemed thin to me now. I should have seen right through them and had I not reacted with too-quick judgement born of emotional overload, I would have recognized the trap in her accusation.

I blinked, and a tear squiggled down my face. "She said you were going to meet her at the Hilton. She left a keycard." Meeting his eyes, I silently pleaded for understanding. "But Ian showed up right after I did. He said he got a message from you. He thought he was meeting you at the hotel." Pissed at myself, I dashed away the moisture collecting on my cheeks. "She set us up, and I fell for it. I'm sorry, Master."

With a long sigh, Gage dropped the ball gag and paced a few feet away, turning his back on me for a few seconds that were long enough to ratchet up my anxiety. Eventually, he turned around, dragging both hands down his face. "Did you touch him?"

And that's when I wavered again. The truth clogged my throat, but if I didn't come clean, he'd think the worst. "I…I hugged him."

"Why?"

"I was shocked to see him, and…" My stomach turned, making me ill. My reasons were unimportant to Gage, as I had no business laying a finger on Ian Kaplan.

"And?" he prompted.

"Please don't make me say it."

"You were happy to see him alive." His tone was so matter-of-fact that I wondered if he had mind-reading capabilities.

"Yes, Master." God, how my cheeks burned with shame. I shouldn't feel guilty for finding joy in knowing that someone I cared about was alive and healthy, but I did. "I'm sorry, but it's the truth."

"I appreciate your honesty, baby."

"But?"

"But I'm hurt as fuck. When will you learn that you need to come to *me* about things? In fact," he said, walking in a slow circle around me, "I demand it. You come to me, or you get punished. This wouldn't have happened if you'd trusted me."

"I know, Master." I hung my head, misery fisting my gut. "Please don't take away my phone and car. I'm begging you. I'll take any other punishment you wish to give."

"Yes, you will, because you don't have a choice. As for your privileges, we'll discuss that later."

His words crashed over me like a frigid wave, and they were a much-needed wake-up call because everything he gave me was a privilege and not a right. I had none in this marriage—in this fucked up union I agreed to every damn day by staying. There were no victims here—only obsessed people who knew the fucked-uppedness of their relationship and stuck through it anyway.

"Get up." He held out a hand and pulled me to my feet, and as he escorted me to the other end of the room, near his wall of pain-inducing implements, I experienced a new level of fear. A piece of equipment I hadn't seen before had been stowed away in the corner of the room, hidden underneath a black cloth.

He whipped the material off and revealed a wooden stockade. "I had this delivered earlier this week while you were out with Simone."

"What is it, Master?"

"A device designed to position you for anal discipline."

Holy shit, the thing looked medieval. It had an upright panel that tilted toward the surface at a slight angle. Holes for wrists and ankles sat top and bottom, and a cutout for where I assumed my bottom would fit took up the space front and center. He was going to lock me in that contraption and objectify my ass. Instinctively, I backed up a few feet.

"What are you going to do to me, Master?"

"To put it mildly, I'm going to make it *very* difficult for you to sit."

My body shook, and I tasted blood from gnawing my lower lip.

"Come here," he ordered.

My feet refused to move, and my heart refused to stop pounding in my ears.

"Baby, don't fight me on this. You won't win." Gage stormed the few feet between us and propelled me forward. His hold on me was harsh and absolute, but his voice had softened, sending a gentle breeze onto my fiery terror.

My submission was the key to everything—freedom, forgiveness, fortitude.

Of my own free will, I slipped my sweaty palm into his and let him help me climb onto his new torture device. "H-how do you want me, Master?"

The sexy timbre of his voice cast me under a spell as he explained how to position myself. I settled horizontally onto the bench, my cheek to the wood, and spread my knees before tucking them underneath my abdomen. The wood was surprisingly smooth against my skin.

"Higher," he murmured, fitting a palm under my bottom and pushing upward. Then he pulled his hand away and ordered me to scoot all the way back until my ass protruded through the cutout in the wood.

A mechanism sounded, and I gripped the edge of the table as Gage fastened my ankles below my exposed ass and pussy. With surprising gentleness, he pulled my arms behind my back and secured my wrists in the openings situated at the top. It was a humiliating position, a variation of a kneeling hogtie—only more painful because a single panel of wood trapped my ankles, ass, and wrists behind me. I'd never felt so helpless, so immobile with my bottom exposed to the chilly air of the basement and cheeks spread in preparation for what I knew was going to be an excruciating punishment. My ass was well and truly stuck within the confines of his stockade. And undoubtedly fucked.

"Before we begin, let's get something straight, Kayla. Forgiving you earlier this year wasn't easy, but it was necessary because I refuse to live without you. My brother, on the other hand, will never be forgiven. He knew better than to come back."

"Please, Master. He's not—"

"You are not to beg tonight," Gage interrupted. "You're going to accept this punishment without a single 'please' or 'stop.' Do you understand?"

"Yes, Master." I did understand. Begging for mercy was not only pointless, but it was humiliating.

"Ian knew the consequences of coming back. His decision to go against my wishes was not in the scope of your control—I understand that—but you will be punished for it regardless." He walked out of sight, and I felt the heat of his body at my backside.

He slipped two fingers inside me, then forced his thumb into my dry asshole. "This is going to hurt. But I think you need a painful reminder of who you belong to." He paused a beat. "Who owns you, Kayla?"

"You do, Master."

"We both know I don't need your permission to punish you, but I'm asking for it anyway. Do you give me permission to punish you as I wish?"

Oh, what a sadistic question. I considered saying no, mostly because I was curious if he'd honor my wishes for a change. I faltered for a mere second, and that was all it took to come to the conclusion that he would *not* bow to what I wanted. If I went against him, even verbally, he would still go through with the punishment, only he'd do his worst.

But what if I were wrong? What if accepting his firm hand and sadistic need for retribution was the only way past what I'd done today? I'd kneeled with the intention of asking for forgiveness in Gage's language.

So I answered in the most honest yet harrowing way I could. "You have my trust and permission, Master."

I heard him exhale—a telling sound indeed. And as he placed one palm on my left ass cheek, rubbing some warmth into my skin, I knew I'd given the right answer.

"Your submission is like a drug, baby. It's precious,

and it means the world to me." He landed a smack that not only smarted, but it fucking turned me on. Then he repeated the stinging swat on my other cheek. Back and forth, he continued the spanking, escalating in velocity and strength until he had me tensing with each calculated swat.

Gage wasn't doing this to punish in the painful sense; he wanted me aroused before he went haywire on my backside.

God, why did I love this sadistic prick so much?

"I love how vulnerable you are right now. You are physically incapable of denying me anything. I can beat your ass for as long as I wish, fuck it for as long as I want. Or," he said, his tone dropping to a dangerous level, "punish it until you lose the ability to scream."

My blood turned to ice. "Master?" I said, a mere whimper.

"No begging. I won't warn you again. Next time you disobey me, I'll gag you." He commenced with the spanking for a while longer, working me into a quivering mass of arousal. "Your cunt is leaking all over the wood."

"I'm sorry, Master." Closing my eyes, I gnawed on my lip.

"Don't be. I want you on edge, your cunt dripping in shame even as you tense from not knowing what I'll do next." He rubbed his palms over my smarting backside, then he inserted a finger into my disloyal cunt. "Are you wondering how I'm going to hurt you?"

"Yes," I moaned, wishing I could squirm from his touch, or at the very least, block it out. I'd give anything to have control over my body, to be able to deny him in some small way.

"We're going to go slow and steady, working our way through each implement one by one." His hands disappeared from my backside, and he came into view, stopping in my line of sight to work the buttons of his white dress shirt free. The material slid over his shoulders and down his arms, and he laid it over the arm of a chair before unbuckling his belt.

Swish.

The belt slipped free of his pant loops. "After your ass is nice and red, and beautifully welted, we'll move on to the punishment of your hole. I made you wet first to ready you for punishment because I do intend to make you scream."

Tears threatened to flood my eyes. I blinked them back with sheer willpower. Crying would not endear me to him right now. He didn't want crying or begging—only my absolute acceptance of his discipline.

And right then I understood more than ever how his mind was wired. Accepting pain equaled disowning my past with his brother. I ached to wrap my arms around him and tell him how much I loved him. Tell him I'd never betray him again. But Gage didn't need that. A normal man might. For Gage, true apology lay in the steadfast way I took his strikes. My redemption lay in an ass left so red and beaten and welted that the mere act of sitting would be impossible. So I apologized in the only way he understood—I gritted my teeth and silently accepted the first strike of his belt.

11. SEVERITY

The smoldering ash of Gage's retribution encased my backside. He wasn't counting tonight, which made receiving the lashes of his belt even more challenging because I didn't know when they'd stop.

I thought they'd never stop.

Through the strikes, I refrained from sobbing, bit back every moan of pain, every whimper at the bone-chilling *crack* of leather against flesh. But then he moved on to a paddle riddled with holes, and I couldn't help but let loose a whimper. The real test came with the cane, never mind the bullwhip because I couldn't begin to comprehend making it through that, and I prayed to anyone listening that Gage would stop after the cane.

Crack!

"Ahhh! Plea—" I choked on the plea, horrified at the thought of starting from square one.

He walked to the front of the bench and stared down at me. I could only imagine what I must look like—blotchy skin from the tears that finally escaped, mouth open to pant through the pain, and strands of hair caught in my eyes, stuck to my cheek from sweat and saliva.

His soft, warm fingers brushed my hair back from my face. "What could you have done differently?"

"What do you mean, Master?"

"At the hotel when you first saw him. Tell me what you could have done differently that might have saved you this level of punishment."

"I could've called you."

"You *should* have called me, at the very least."

"I know, Master. I'm sorry I let you down."

"You disappointed me," he said, brushing a thumb over my lips, "but you didn't let me down. You weren't unfaithful, and this punishment will ensure you stay loyal to me until the day you die. I won't allow you to stumble again."

He disappeared once more, and the next blow to my ass stole my breath. I couldn't make a sound if I tried. His evil cane cut across my ass in sharp lines, one on top of the other, and I knew from experience that those wounds would stay with me for a while, above and below the surface.

Some time later, the cane clattered to the floor. He'd been dropping implements left and right, which was so unlike him. He reached for the bullwhip, and that's when I slipped up. That's when a sob escaped, and I cried out a plea in the form of his favorite title.

"*Master...*" God, how I choked on the word, but I almost threw up at the thought of his whip landing on top of the welts from the cane.

He came to stand in front of me again, bullwhip held in a white-knuckled grip. "Do we need to start over?"

"No! I want the bullwhip!" Desperation strung those words together, screeched in a high-pitched tone.

"Don't lie to me. We both know you hate the bullwhip."

"I'm sorry, Master. Don't make me start over again." My voice was near to pleading, which terrified me even more. "I just want this to be over."

And that was the honest fucking truth.

He leaned down, and his lips claimed my mouth. The kiss was too brief; a fleeting moment of bliss that seemed more like a dream in my current mental state. He pulled away, and I ached to do something—anything—to bring his mouth back. As long as he kissed me, he wouldn't hurt me anymore.

"This will be over soon, baby. Then we can move on."

Soon was not the word I'd use. His inner sadist had taken control, and he wasn't likely to unhand the reins anytime soon. Gage lost himself a little more to that monster with each minute that passed. And there were a lot of them. Minute after minute after minute of his bullwhip cracking through the air before it thrashed my thoroughly abused ass.

Forget composure. Forget acceptance. I screamed and cried and even cursed.

"I hate you!" I sobbed.

"I don't blame you for saying that right now," he said, a note of hurt tainting his voice as he brought the whip onto my ass once again.

"Fuck you! How can you be so cruel?" Hell, I lashed out in any form he'd allow. As long as I wasn't begging for it to stop, he let me throw my agony-induced tantrums, similar to a woman in the throes of labor during the horrendous stage of transition. And that's where I was—out of my mind with pain and so high on adrenaline that reality was a nebulous concept viewed through warped glass.

"You don't love me," I whined.

"I love you too much."

Whack!

"This isn't love!" My words echoed off the walls, and only then did I realize I'd screamed them.

"You're probably right, but it's the only way I know how to love."

Whack!

"Oh God! Fuck! Fuck! It hurts, Gage. It hurts!"

"It's supposed to hurt."

"No," I moaned, unable to find the strength to keep screaming at him. "Love isn't supposed to hurt like this."

He dropped the whip, and as that fucker hit the ground, echoing with hope through my ears, I'd never experienced so much relief. I would never, ever cross this man again. Ever.

"Thank God," I mumbled.

"We're not done yet."

But I didn't care. He could stick his thumb up my ass all night long if he wanted, because that was a hundred times better than getting spanked, lashed with a belt, beat with a paddle, struck with a cane, and tormented with a bullwhip. I was in no hurry to examine my backside in a mirror.

Gage opened a drawer and pulled out a rod-like toy of some sort, and that's when it hit me that he wasn't planning to use his thumb. The instrument was long and fat, bigger than his cock, and one end had a rounded head designed for penetration.

Begging for mercy was on the tip of my tongue, so I bit it instead.

"I want anal sex to be amazing for you. To achieve that goal it's going to take time and patience, and harsh anal punishments to remind you of how pleasurable my cock can be in comparison. You're going to learn the differences between anal penetration for pleasure and punishment."

"It's too big, Master."

He pressed a finger to my lips. "I allowed you to cry and insult me during the first portion of your discipline. But now you will remain quiet and reflect on the behavior that got you here. Don't make me start over, Kayla."

I clenched my teeth, knowing that I'd summon the strength to get through this. I was stronger than he realized...or maybe he did realize the extent of my resilience. Maybe that's why he pushed so hard—because he knew I could bounce back from his shit. Maybe I was the one woman capable of surviving Gage Channing's all-consuming sadism.

But as he inched that steel shaft up my ass, using a minimal amount of lube, I wondered if maybe they should just toss me in a loony bin and throw away the key.

12. AFTER CARE

Warm water sluiced over my head, spraying from the multiple shower heads, and dripped off my nose, running over my breasts before sliding down my spread legs. Facing the shower wall, thighs open to my husband's questing hands, and arms over my head with my palms flat against the tile, I bit my lip as he washed me...and coaxed me to arousal.

But my mind replayed his vile use of that anal rod. He'd punished my ass slowly, first inching the thing in, allowing my anus to stretch and burn around the intrusion for a few minutes before he removed it.

Then he'd insert it again.

He must have penetrated me with that rod a dozen times—as many times as it took to lose a whole hour or more to his sick punishment of my hole.

"I'm proud of you," he said, his fingers moving between my thighs.

"I'm pissed at you," I bit back. Even as I sassed him, uncaring of the consequences at this point, my legs betrayed me and opened wider to accommodate his touch. I didn't know whether to lash out in anger, sob from the despair fisting my heart, or come all over his teasing fingers. Leaning my forehead against the wall, I pushed my ass toward him, an invitation to touch me deeper.

"How do you do this to me?"

"Do what, baby?"

"Make me want to come after everything you just did."

"It's a talent of mine," he said, finally slipping his fingers inside me.

"I'm still pissed at you, Master."

"That's okay. You're entitled to your emotions, Kayla. I put your ass through the ringer."

"I'm scared to look at it."

In response, he brushed his fingers over my stinging backside. "Your ass is gorgeous. I was careful not to draw too much blood, but you really won't be able to sit for a couple of days. I wasn't kidding about that."

"Can I speak freely, Master?" The last thing I wanted was to push too hard and earn an additional punishment.

"You may."

His gentle manner was my undoing. I plummeted in a brutal mood swing more powerful than his strikes, and a sob wrenched from my soul. "How can you love me and hurt me like this? How? I don't understand."

"I told you a long time ago that I'm a bastard. But I'm your bastard, Kayla. And I do love you. I love you more fiercely than the burn in your ass right now, with so much loyalty that I'd gladly kill anyone who hurt you."

"But *you* hurt me."

"And I'm the only one who ever will." He thrust his fingers in a steady rhythm, propelling me to that glorious edge I craved. Oh, how I needed to jump off right now.

I moaned and groaned, my hands balled into fists against the tile. "Master, please."

"Please, what?" He blew a warm breath over my bottom, and I liked that he was on his haunches behind me, practically worshipping the handiwork of his sadism while simultaneously gifting me pleasure.

"Can I come, Master?"

"You may not."

"Grrr!" Bumping my forehead on the tile, I gritted my teeth to keep from slinging hateful words at him.

"You're still being punished. You don't get to come during a punishment. You know that."

Still being punished…

A flash of Katherine on her knees, her slutty mouth inches from his cock, sprang to mind, causing my body to go rigid. But recalling his words truly iced my heart.

If you ever touch another man again, I'll not only fuck her, but I'll do it in front of you.

I hadn't betrayed him, but a hug could be construed as touching another man. "Are you going to…?" Suddenly, vomit burned my throat.

"Spit it out, Kayla. Whatever it is, don't hold back. That's what got you in trouble in the first place."

"Are you going to use Katherine against me?" Closing my eyes, I failed to breathe as I waited for his answer. But he was quiet, leaving me close to panicking. "Please, Master. I need to know."

"You don't have to worry about Katherine. When I made the threat, I was so angry that I thought I could do it. But fuck, Kayla, I don't think I could ever touch another woman. You're it for me."

The breath I'd been holding whooshed from me in a torrent of relief. "You're it for me too. I need you to know that."

His lack of response worried me. He stopped caressing between my legs, but still, he didn't say anything.

"Gage, I mean it. Please know that."

"You don't have any feelings for him?"

"Not like I used to." Gage had purged my love for Ian the instant he'd sentenced me to that cage. "Honestly, after I got over the shock of seeing him, I was more worried about how you'd react."

He rose behind me, pressing his erection against my sore ass, and gripped my hair in an uncompromising fist. "Swear to me that he means nothing."

"He means nothing."

Gage pulled on my hair, angling my head so he could claim my mouth. The spray from the shower misted over our faces, wetting our lips as we came together in an open-mouthed kiss that sucked the will right out of my bones.

I whimpered against his lips, needing more...so much more.

He inched back with a groan. "I want in your ass so badly right now."

My breath hitched, and I turned horrified eyes on him. I could not, for the fucking life of me, comprehend taking his cock right now. Not with the way my ass burned.

"Relax, baby," he whispered, brushing his mouth over mine again. "I know you're in pain, so I'll settle for your mouth instead." He let out a breath that shivered against my well-kissed lips. "On your knees."

His command, spoken soft and low yet full of authority, shot straight to my pussy. I turned around and kneeled before him, then eagerly accepted his cock into my mouth. He pushed his hands into my hair, brushing the wet strands from my eyes.

"Baby, look at me."

God, he was beautiful. Dark hair drenched, blue eyes more startling than usual—I was helpless against this man, especially when he gave in to the speck of tenderness hiding inside his sadistic soul. Instead of grabbing my hair and ramming his cock down my throat, like he normally would, he combed his fingers through my hair as he slipped in and out of my mouth.

Intense heat flared between my thighs, and I whimpered around his shaft, tongue massaging the softness of his head.

Propping an arm against the tile, he groaned deep in his throat as he gazed down at me in wonder. "Don't stop doing that with your tongue. It feels unbelievable." His mouth flattened into a determined line. "You're being such a good girl. Fuck, I want to make you come into next year."

But he wouldn't. Gage had many sides to him, but he rarely wavered on punishment, and holding my orgasm at bay was part of it.

I sucked him to release, accepting every last drop, and despite the desire blazing between my thighs, I felt mostly…content. We finished washing up, then he towel-dried my skin, paying careful attention to his favorite areas before instructing me to bend over the counter.

"I love marking you like this." He opened a tube of cream and squirted a dollop into his palm. "Your ass was made for me." As he gently rubbed the soothing balm into my skin, I wondered how he'd managed to coach me through fear, then anger before molding me into a content pile of skin and bones, subservient to his wants and needs, and pliant in his hands.

I had no answers and no chance to mull over his sorcery-like mojo any longer. He scooped me up in his arms and carried me upstairs to our bedroom, winding a path through the darkness to our bed. He set me on my feet before turning down the covers.

"Grab your ankles."

I did so without question. He probed my pussy, gliding his devious fingers through the evidence of just how fundamentally screwed my body was. And even in the darkness, his face cast in shadow from my bent over position, I knew he was pleased.

He'd punished my ass to his liking and had nearly brought me to orgasm enough times to leave me drenched around his fingers. Gage Channing's work for the day was done. His self-satisfied sigh confirmed it as he pulled me into bed beside him, yanking my stinging ass snug against his thighs. And though he didn't voice the words, his long sigh told me all I needed to know.

That night, I fell asleep wrapped in his forgiveness and love.

13. TENDER MERCY

Gage was having my masquerade gown designed. He'd stuffed most of my closet with custom made clothing from some of the top designers in the world. Every button and bead had been added down to his specifications. If I were going to be his trophy wife, then he'd outfit me like one. Considering the charity ball was less than a week away, he'd put a rush on my dress, no doubt paying a ridiculously high premium.

"Not even a teensy little hint?" I needled him, lying on top of his body because I still couldn't sit without pain after the punishment he'd issued the previous night.

"You'll see it Friday night." His warm hands drifted over my naked backside, his caresses downright hypnotic. The same hands that delivered excruciating pain were also the same hands that moved over my skin in a way that made me feel treasured and loved. I buried my nose in the crook of his neck, suddenly overcome.

"What's wrong, baby?"

"I don't know. Nothing." Maybe I was having a

woman moment. In fact, that particular curse was due any day.

"Are you worried you'll lose your privileges?"

The issue had crossed my mind a few times, but I couldn't say I'd thought about it tonight. Not with the way he'd...*God*...

He'd made love to me.

"You had honest intentions, Kayla, so I won't punish you further by taking your car or phone away."

"Thank you, Master."

His chest went still as if he were holding his breath. "Are you still angry with me?"

"No, Master. I just wish..." I swallowed hard before forging ahead, knowing he'd want me to share what troubled me. "I wish we had more moments like these."

Moments where we lost an endless amount of time, tangled as one in the darkness of our bedroom, bodies swallowed in the sheets. These kinds of nights were few and far between.

He grabbed my hips, pulled, and urged me to my knees. "I vow to you right now that we'll have more of these moments, Kayla." Nudging my opening with his cock, he shuddered a breath into my hair. "Ride me."

"Again?"

"Did I stutter?"

With a slow downward thrust, I sheathed his cock.

"Look at me," he said, fisting my hair with both hands. He pulled my head up by force, too impatient for me to unbury my face on my own. "Don't forget that I'm calling the shots here. You being on top means nothing."

I wouldn't dare to be so foolish. He'd allowed me the sacred privilege of control twice since I'd known him—only because I'd tied him to the bed in a role reversal he probably still regretted to this day. But truthfully, Gage had wielded power over me both times, because that's who he was. Even gagged and tied, he'd owned me.

And he always would.

"I don't want fast and hard," he said, fingers loosening in my hair. "Fuck me slowly."

Undulating my hips, I dropped my forehead against his, and our gazes locked together as surely as our bodies did. His breath became my own, and the adoration in his eyes hit me square in the chest, stealing my life-force.

"I have no fucking words for how good you feel right now," he said, sliding his hands along my cheeks. Gage could do tender when he wanted to—when he wasn't preoccupied with taking me by force or delivering a punishment.

Sometimes, he loved me like a normal man.

Fuck, I was going to cry and ruin this moment. I shuttered my eyes against the threat of tears, but it was too late. He swiped at the moisture creeping out from underneath my lashes.

"Baby, eyes on me."

Exhaling the sob I'd been holding back, I opened my eyes, and confusion overshadowed his blue gaze.

"Why are you crying?"

"I don't know." And I truly didn't. Maybe his tenderness on the tail of such brutality did me in. Or maybe I just needed him too much, and a tiny part of me wept over the hold he had on me.

Cradling my cheeks, he nipped at my lips before drawing me into a kiss that destroyed me. Our tongues came together in sync with our bodies. The salt of my tears infused our taste buds with a spectrum of emotions, cleansing us of past hurts. We kissed and fucked in perfect harmony, each note falling into place, every high and low executed with mastery.

He let go of my face with a groan, grabbed my hips, and yanked me down until I took his cock to the hilt. "I'll never get enough. Your body enchants me—"

Another upward thrust hit my G-spot, and I cried out with a delicious shudder.

"Your smile lights my world, baby. And your stubbornness…hell, you can't help but challenge the bastard in me." As if to punctuate his words, he dug his fingers into my tender ass. "I know loving me isn't easy, but you do it so damn well."

The tears would never stop at this rate. I clutched his hair and fucked the *fuck* out of him, mindless of the way his hands gouged my red and welted flesh. His touch guided me, punished me, but above all else, he held me to him with fierce possession.

He'd never let me go, and the certainty of that knowledge swaddled my heart in absolution.

"No more doubts," I cried, lips damp against his skin.

"No more doubts," he agreed, then he sucked in a sharp breath. "You're making me lose my shit. I'm gonna come, and if you don't come with me, I'll spank the fuck out of your ass."

That was all I needed—the mental picture of his authoritative hand on my bottom. I fell apart within the confines of his embrace...no, we fell apart in each other's arms, groaning and grunting and moaning incoherent nothings as we grasped for that wondrous high together.

14. O.M.G. AGAIN

The week began with torrential rain. I found the downpour symbolic as if Mother Nature was urging us to wash away the darker aspects of our histories and focus on the future instead. And the future held a bright new beginning, in more ways than one.

For the first time since we'd married, Gage allowed me to find purpose in something other than motherhood or being a wife and slave. He'd hired me on as his personal assistant again, this time on a part-time basis. For the first two days, I worked at his side until noon, at which point he sent me home to perform my wifely duties. Housekeeping, shopping, and meal preparation were still my responsibilities, though if I started working more hours at Channing Enterprises, he'd allow me to hire help at home.

But for now, my new job was on a conditional basis until I proved that I could keep up with my duties. Everything was going smoothly until Wednesday when life slapped me in the face with a huge wake-up call.

I'd just walked into the foyer when the lunch I'd had with Gage turned in my gut. I barely made it to the bathroom before losing the contents of my stomach. As I held onto the gleaming porcelain, heaving for all I was worth, I could no longer deny it. Getting sick all the time wasn't due to stress, and the stomach bug that had visited Eve was long gone.

This was something else. Something I couldn't bring myself to hope for just yet…until I ran the calculations in my head and realized I was late.

I should have called Gage, but when I picked up my cell, Simone's number was the one my fingers dialed. Late or not, I wasn't about to get Gage's hopes up for nothing. A piss stick would have to show me two lines first.

Then I'd tell him…if I had anything to tell at all.

Simone answered on the fifth ring. "What's up?"

"Are you working today? I was hoping we could get together."

A few seconds of quiet passed. "Ian told me he ran into you," she finally said, hesitancy lacing her tone. "I'm sorry I didn't tell you about us."

Her words caught me off-guard. "That's not why I'm calling." The incident with Ian seemed like weeks ago instead of days, considering everything that was going through my mind now.

"Oh," she said, sounding surprised. "You seem a little upset, so I thought…"

"I'm not upset about you and Ian." Sure, I shared enough history with Ian that the idea of him moving on wasn't the easiest thing to face, but the pain was but a phantom ping—an ache stamped on my heart like a fading tattoo. "I was actually hoping you'd want to help me shop for…Halloween costumes."

Not pregnancy tests. No siree.

Besides, I did need to find a costume for Eve. I was fairly certain Gage would give me permission to leave the house if I told him I was shopping for Halloween costumes. "I need to find something for Eve."

"Okay." But doubt tinged her voice. "My shift ends in an hour."

I told her where to meet me, then she hung up without a goodbye, which was a very Simone-like thing to do. Two hours later, we were sorting through the racks at a costume shop in comfortable silence.

"Are you sure you're okay?" Simone asked, breaking the quiet between us. Okay, so comfortable wasn't the word I'd use, but I hadn't realized my distress was that noticeable, and she obviously mistook it for unhappiness over her new relationship status.

"I'm fine," I said, fingering the lace on an Elsa ensemble—which was *so* two years ago according to Eve. "Why?"

Simone gave a sarcastic quirk of her brow. "You've been touching that hideous costume for the last three minutes while staring into space."

Expelling a sigh, I let Elsa's cheap and scratchy blue skirt slip from my fingers. It was now or never. "I need to buy a pregnancy test." My emotions were all over the fucking place. The threat of tears burned my eyes, but on the opposite end of the spectrum, my belly fluttered with the possibility of a positive sign.

A literal fucking positive sign.

Cool it, Kayla. It's probably nothing.

"Hey, this is great news…isn't it?" She frowned. "You've been trying to get knocked up with that devil's spawn for…well, for what seems like forever."

"Gage doesn't know I'm buying a test."

"*Oooh*," she said, drawing out the word. "You're worried he's going to turn you over his knee for going *mum's-the-word?*"

"Something like that." A spanking over his knee was foreplay. More than anything, I hated the thought of him finding out about the test if it ended up being negative. I wasn't sure I could handle the disappointment in his eyes. He tried to hide it, but after living most of his adult life believing he was unable to have children, only to find out the diagnosis had been incorrect, I knew how much he wanted this.

A baby of his own.

Katherine had robbed him of Conner's early childhood years, and Eve had been three-years-old when he'd forced his way into our lives. He wanted this badly… possibly more than I did.

"You know how I feel about that man," Simone said, "but I think he'd want to go through this with you, no matter the results."

"I know you're right."

"What's the problem then?"

"I need to be sure before I tell him."

She grabbed my arm and escorted me to a bench

designated for shoppers to try on shoes. "And you'll have an answer soon, but first you need to take a few deep breaths and calm down." She settled beside me, and I buried my face in my hands, drawing shallow, hot breaths from between my palms.

"We'll go to the pharmacy together, okay?"

"What if I'm not?"

"But what if you are?" she said. "Only one way to find out."

And that's when I realized that both outcomes equally terrified me—a reaction I hadn't expected. I figured I'd be overjoyed at the possibility of being pregnant, but now that I had a real chance I considered things I hadn't thought of until now.

Like the fact that I was prone to miscarriages and tubal pregnancies.

Or how my slave duties would make carrying a baby difficult. How would I handle Gage's rituals and punishments on top of pregnancy? And then, after the baby arrived...would I be too exhausted to want sex, let alone kneel on command, ready to please?

Simone pulled me to my feet. "Okay, no more freaking out about this. Let's buy a test and get an answer." She ushered me through the mall and to the parking lot with a purposeful stride.

Simone was a life savor that afternoon. She ran into the pharmacy and came out fifteen minutes later with half a dozen tests, each one advertised at being the best, most accurate on the market. Somehow, she knew I wasn't ready to go home yet, so she drove straight to her house.

Now I found myself pacing in front of her bathroom door, the bag of tests in my hands, terrified to hope. My heartbeat was a wild beast behind my breastbone. I should have called Gage. Deep down, I knew I was going about this the wrong way, but the idea of taking a test while he eagerly waited was too upsetting. Once again, vomit pushed its way into my throat, and I bolted into the bathroom and threw up for the second time that day. The situation felt too reminiscent of another day.

The vomiting. The test. The reminder of Gage's reaction afterward.

I curled into a ball next to the porcelain God and sobbed. Taking the test wasn't even important—it would only confirm what I already knew in my heart. The impossible had happened. My remaining ovary had produced an egg, and Gage...

His reaction would be so different from last time, but in that moment, all I could hear were the echoes of his rage. The accusations and hatred. Forgiving was easy. Forgetting was harder.

"What can I do?" Simone set a hand on my shoulder, her touch light and gentle as if I might jump out of my skin. I pulled myself upright.

"I'm pregnant. I know I am."

"You won't know for sure until you take a test."

"I'm scared to."

"I thought you wanted to have a baby?"

"I do!"

"Then why are you falling apart before you've even

pissed on a stick?"

"I don't know! I guess it's…Gage didn't handle it so well last time."

"But he's onboard now, right?" She gentled her tone, infusing her words with the power to coax.

"Yeah."

Simone grabbed my hand and dragged me to my feet. "No point in having a breakdown until you at least confirm it." She picked up the bag I'd dropped and pushed it into my shaking hands. "I'll be right outside the door."

I gave a solemn nod as if headed to a firing squad instead of taking a test that was bound to give me news I'd been hoping to receive for months. The next three minutes were the longest of my life—at least that's what it felt like when I finally picked up the stick and read the results.

Two lines.

15. COME CLEAN

Gage slid the razor over his jaw and down the side of his neck in hypnotic strokes, erasing his five o'clock shadow. I sat on the edge of the tub and rubbed jasmine scented lotion into my smooth legs. I liked watching him do mundane things. Standing barefoot with nothing but a towel wrapped around his waist, he didn't come across nearly as intimidating as he normally did.

Until he turned that steel blue gaze on me in the mirror.

I didn't know what propelled me to kneel behind him, my hands tugging at the terrycloth around his waist. The towel floated to the floor, and I wrapped my fingers around his cock. It only took a few strokes to get him hard. He dropped the razor onto the counter.

"What are you doing?"

I didn't often take the initiative. He'd conditioned me to follow his lead, and that was a hard lesson to break.

"Serving you, Master." Swiping my thumb over the head of his cock, I bit my lower lip, hiding a smile at the bead of moisture on my fingers.

"Did I give you permission to grope me?"

"No, Master."

He chuckled, but as soon as I stroked the length of him, his laughter turned to a deep-throated groan. "You're being very bad. You interrupted my shaving, Kayla," he said, but his tone teased rather than admonished. "Now I have no choice but to punish your mouth." He whirled and had my head between his hands before I had a chance to move out of reach. As he pushed between my lips, his gaze roamed my face, as if he were searching for the answer to my out-of-character behavior.

"You've been quiet tonight, and now you're on your knees playing with my cock of your own accord. Something is obviously going on here." He thrust deeper, ensuring I couldn't answer him.

And that's when things took a turn for the worst. My gag reflex kicked in, stronger than ever, and I jerked my head back. But he moved with me, wordlessly forbidding me to pull away. Gagging was a huge turn-on for him, and he wasn't about to give me any slack.

"While I fuck your mouth, why don't you consider telling me what's on your mind?" He paused for a moment, a dark brow arched. "Something *is* on your mind, right?" Ceasing his thrusts, he allowed me a quick nod of my head.

Would my entire pregnancy be like this? Struggling with the side-effects of growing a baby inside my body while he took his pleasure from me? All evening I'd worried over how to tell him, but suddenly, I wanted answers first.

He moved his hips in a lazy circle, keeping his cock buried deep in my mouth, and hitting the back of my throat with each rotation. His eyes deepened to my favorite shade of indigo. Sometimes, that hue was a warning, but more often than not, it was a sign of his raging arousal.

Gage was possibly the most passionate man I'd ever met.

With a grunt, he pushed further into my throat, and I gagged so hard my eyes burned from unshed tears. My belly roiled—a sure sign I was in trouble if I didn't get him off pronto. Renewing my efforts, I worked his shaft with my tongue and lips, hoping against hope that it would be enough to make him come. I wasn't sure how much longer I could stand his cock trapped in my throat, no matter how much I loved making him go wild with my mouth.

And this was why I needed to tell him, or at the very least, open a conversation about the what-ifs of pregnancy.

He withdrew without warning, causing my lips to make a popping sound. Then he bent over and hefted me to my feet with two hands under my shoulders. He spun us around, lifted me onto the counter, and buried his half-shaven face between my legs, smearing shaving cream on my skin in the process. My elbows hit the counter hard, but I didn't give a fuck. Not as long as he kept flicking his tongue over my clit like that.

"Master…feels so good."

He lifted his head. "I lick, you talk."

My head fell back against the mirror. "About what?" His wondrous tongue derailed my train of thought.

"Tell me what's bothering you, or I'll stop." Again, he lifted his head and stared at me, brows narrowed over eyes that saw too much. "You haven't been yourself all afternoon. I know when something is off."

"I've been thinking about…" He darted his tongue into my opening, and I gripped the edge of the counter with white-knuckled fingers. "Oh, God. Don't stop."

"Then finish what you were going to say. You've been thinking about what?"

"What if…what if I do get pregnant?"

As soon as I said those words, he backed away completely, and I lamented the loss of the heights he would have surely sent me to. But the way he watched me, with a mixture of suspicion and hope, told me that our oral session was over. Reluctantly, I slid to my feet.

"What do you mean *what if?*" He folded his arms, and somehow he didn't look ridiculous standing buck naked like that. If anything, he seemed more formidable. "As far as I knew there was only *when*. Are you trying to tell me something, Kayla?"

"No! I just never gave it much thought until now, but…"

"But what?" His voice rose, on the edge of anger. He was taking this all wrong. Or I wasn't explaining myself in the right way.

"How will you treat me during the pregnancy, or after

the baby is born?" Considering the what-ifs—the ones I'd never given much thought to because getting pregnant seemed like a pipe dream—were making me nauseous.

Either that or it was morning sickness.

"I've done research, Kayla. You need to trust me to know what is safe and what isn't."

"I'm not just talking about safety. I'm talking about… about what I want." I wrung my hands before forging ahead. "If I were to get pregnant, I'd want more freedom. And once the baby arrives…" I gulped, kicking myself for the slip-up. "I mean I can't comprehend taking care of a newborn and kneeling at your feet daily, or taking your belt or…or your anal punishments. Gage, I'd need you to tone it down."

A tick went off in his jaw, and for a second I thought he'd figured me out. "You sound like you don't want a baby. First your talk the other night about how it might not be in the cards for us, and now this?" He took a step toward me, but my back hit the edge of the counter, leaving me no room to escape.

"Have you been taking birth control pills behind my back? Is that why you're not getting pregnant?"

"What?" My eyes widened. "No! These are just things…I've just been giving this stuff some thought lately."

"Well here's all you need to know. I'm your Master, and I *will* take care of you. You might not always like my methods, but I won't hurt you beyond what you can handle."

"What if I don't want to 'handle' it while pregnant or

taking care of a newborn?" My voice climbed higher with every word, and I regretted it immediately because I knew what he was after before he disappeared from the bathroom. A few moments later, he returned with the ever-dreaded ball gag clutched in his fist.

Shaking my head, I flattened my lips together in pure defiance. "I'm sorry I lost my cool, but this is serious, Gage. We need to talk about this."

"I'll talk. You're going to listen." He pressed the gag to my lips, but I batted his hand—and the gag—away. Even as I did so, I was horrified by my actions. Not because they were out of line, but because they were out of line according to *his* standards.

"Kayla," he warned, once again coming at me with that horrid gag.

"Please, Master. Can't we just talk about—"

"We will talk. We'll talk about anything you want, but *after* you've accepted your punishment."

"What am I being punished for? Will you at least give me a damn reason?"

His mouth formed an indomitable line. "The way you just spoke to me is a fine example of why your disobedient mouth is getting punished."

Why bother protesting? Even if I were ready to tell him about the baby, he wasn't willing to hear me until I took my discipline like the dutiful slave I was. I parted my lips and stretched them around the gag. After he'd tightened the buckle with extra oomph, he ordered me to my knees in the middle of our bedroom.

I did as told, and Gage surprised me by producing a

set of leather cuffs. He secured my wrists behind me, and I had to wonder why. He rarely restrained me anymore— he didn't have to. A slight chill stirred by body as he walked in a slow circle around me.

"I may be your husband, but this is not a normal marriage. You knew going in that I would have absolute authority over your life, your body, and your decisions." Completing another circle, he came to a stop in front of me. "You have no control here, Kayla. And though I love your feisty spirit—God, I truly do—I won't hesitate to put you in your place, pregnant or not."

He cocked his head to the side. "And this is your place—on your knees, naked, bound, and gagged. Your place is on all fours, offering your cunt and asshole whenever I wish. Your *place*," he said, raising his voice, "is in any damn position I see fit with your mouth wide open and eager to please me."

Sliding his fingers under my chin, he forced my head up, eyes on him. "There is only one path to freedom, and it's one I know you'll never take. I've made sure of it."

Everything he said was true, and it rose inside me, an insidious truth I couldn't deny. He'd manipulated and molded me, trained and conditioned me. My will was strong and always present, but he'd somehow rewired it to exist for him.

"I'm not just your husband. I'm your *owner*." Crouching until we were at eye level, he caressed my cheek. "And that takes a lot of trust on your part, but I do realize it's something we're still working on. Your first instinct is to withhold and deceive, and I will not stop until I've eradicated that behavior. You will not doubt me, nor question me, nor fear me. You will learn to submit and serve with total trust."

Something dark and dangerous crossed over his features. "But we aren't there yet, are we? Even after the harsh punishment I put you through last week, you still feel the need to hide things from me."

I shook my head with vehemence.

"The sudden onset of these questions about pregnancy are more than a little suspicious." He pointed to where I kneeled. "Do *not* move from that spot." He hurried back into the bathroom, his stride full of purpose, and my stomach dropped. This couldn't be good. If he planned to search my things for birth control pills that didn't exist…I began to shake. He was going to find the note.

The fucking note I'd forgotten about until now.

To top it off, I was going to choke on my own vomit because I hadn't told him about the baby. That should have been the first thing I'd done this afternoon, as soon as he came through the door.

Instead, I'd stewed and overthought it too much. I'd worried myself into this position. If I'd only been honest, we'd be celebrating right now. But there would be no celebration tonight. How could I expect him to wield his power over me with caution and safety if he didn't have all the facts? No matter the sadistic bastard that lived inside him, I knew he would have never left me gagged, unattended for even a minute if he'd known I was suffering from morning sickness.

Calm down. Deep breaths through the nose.

Breathing deeply and purposefully staved off the nausea. I focused on drawing air in and out of my lungs in a slow and steady rhythm as I waited for him to return. Drawers opened and closed, cupboards squeaked then slammed shut. The unmistakable sound of him rifling through my things filtered to where I knelt. Finally, he appeared in the open doorway of the bathroom, long after my knees had begun to ache from the hard floor, and my burning shoulders slumped.

Entering the bedroom again, Gage came to a stop in front of me. Dread chewed my gut as I saw what he held in his hands. Struggling to dislodge the gag—which was impossible—I whined and shimmied, begging him with my eyes to let me speak.

He took mercy on me. Leaning down, he loosened the strap and pulled the rubber ball from my mouth. But he didn't free my wrists from the cuffs, and that bespoke of the degree of trouble I was in.

"It's not what you think," I hurried to explain, then winced at that particular cliched tripe.

"You're right. It's definitely not what I thought." He began pacing. "I thought maybe you didn't want another child, but you didn't know how to tell me." He clutched my makeup compact in a fist. "I was looking for contraceptives. Instead, I found this."

"Gage—"

He cut me off by swiping a hand through the air. "How long have you been keeping this from me?"

"It doesn't mean anything."

"*How* long?" he demanded, opening the compact before tossing it onto the floor. He balled his fingers around the note, crushing it.

"A few weeks. I would have gotten rid of it last week, but I forgot about it."

Shit. That was *not* the right thing to say. His face darkened, a storm brewing on the horizon.

"Wait, that came out wrong, Master. I meant that the note didn't mean anything to me anymore. I saw that he was okay. In fact, I found out he's dating Simone, and I'm okay with it!" I struggled to my feet, pleading with my eyes for him to understand. "I would have mentioned it, or thrown it away, but I *forgot*."

"How can you just forget something like this?"

"I don't know! I'm sorry, but I did. A lot has happened since that day. You punishing me, starting work with you this week, and then today…"

Oh God. I'd ruined this moment for us. We'd waited so long, and I'd stupidly withheld the news from him, if only for a few hours. But it was long enough for that damn note to spring up and wreak destruction.

"What else, Kayla? What else are you hiding from me?" He towered over me, and I dropped to my knees. Kissed his feet.

"Stop groveling and just tell me."

Lifting my head, I gazed into his eyes—blue orbs filled with anger and hurt and suspicion. "I'm scared to tell you."

For so many reasons, the biggest of which lay wrapped in superstition and the echoes of a painful history. We'd gone down this road before, and it hadn't ended well.

"Jesus, baby. Whatever it is, we'll deal with it together."

"I'm…" I swallowed hard, and maybe it was the speck of tenderness in his expression—the softening of his mouth, and the way he unclenched his hands. The crinkled piece of paper, a souvenir from a painful time that seemed eons ago, floated to the floor, forgotten.

Gage saw my fear, and instead of feeding off it in his usual sadistic way, he empathized. He showed patience and love and even anxiety for what I was about to throw his way. Again.

I'd proven that I was more than capable of letting him down, of wavering when I should stay the course. I kissed his feet once more then smiled up at him through the tears forming in my eyes.

"I'm pregnant."

16. HEARTBEAT

The following morning, Gage got me in to see the best obstetrician that money could buy. We sat side-by-side in the waiting room, hands clasped together. He seemed as nervous as I was. The wait to see the doctor wasn't long, but it seemed to span forever. By the time they called me back, I was sure my blood pressure would rocket through the roof. After the nurse took my vitals and asked a dozen or so questions, she left Gage and me alone with the assurance the doctor would be in shortly.

I hopped onto the table, my ass sliding over the paper, and eyed Gage. He'd unfolded into a chair near the door of the exam room. Between the glaring lights overhead and my lack of sleep the previous night, this whole situation seemed...surreal.

What bothered me most was all the things we hadn't said. After I'd finally gotten the words out about the pregnancy, Gage had flipped through a plethora of reactions, from shocked to elated to disbelieving to... worried.

And that last one set me on edge the most, possibly because it reflected my own fears. Everything was changing so quickly—within my body and in my marriage. I needed his rock solid presence right now. Hell, I even needed his stringent disciplinary measures. They kept me grounded, and I needed that more than ever.

I'd grown accustomed to bowing to his decisions, to depending on him to keep me in line. But a pregnancy… maybe we'd both underestimated the realities that would come with such a life-changing event.

Deep down, I hadn't worried about it much because after those first few months, when it became obvious I wasn't getting pregnant, I hadn't thought it would be an issue we'd have to face.

Turned out I was wrong.

I glanced up and found him staring at me. "What do you need from me, Kayla?"

That was the last thing I'd expected him to say. "I… I'm not sure what you mean."

"You tried talking to me last night about what you'd need, should you become pregnant. I could have handled that conversation a lot better. Instead, I jumped to conclusions, and for that I'm truly sorry. So now I'm asking. Tell me what you need."

I parted my lips, but nothing came out. The best I could do was shrug my shoulders. Problem was, I had no idea what I wanted or needed. My head was still spinning from seeing those two lines yesterday, and the fact that Gage was sitting in that chair, looking so damn lost, just about unhinged me.

"I need you to be *you*," I whispered, my throat constricting. Why was I so upset? Having a baby was a dream come true for us. But neither of us could deny the risks—not with the type of lifestyle we lived and my previous track record with pregnancies.

He rose and crossed to where I sat, legs dangling over the edge of the table. As I drew in a lungful of air, he slid his palms along my cheeks, and it amazed me how gentle he managed to be at times. The tender way he cradled my face was incongruent with his basest self.

"Baby, I'm still the same bastard I was yesterday before you told me. Trust me, there will be times when you wish for more leniency. But damn," he said, caressing my temples with his thumbs. "This is fucking real. It's happening, and I want to do right by you, so tell me what you need."

A breath shuddered from my lips. "I don't know. I thought I'd want things to change between us, but I...I just want you the way you are." A large part of me *needed* to kneel at his feet to feel loved. He cherished me best while on my knees, and I craved that connection with him.

Out of nowhere, tears erupted, and I swiped them away, angry at myself for crying. "I need you to take care of me like you always do. I need the security of being yours."

"That's a given, so why am I sensing a 'but' in there somewhere?"

Was I clinging to a caveat? I searched within myself and found the perpetual need to be owned by him, but also to have a piece of me that I could call my own. The strikes of his implements wouldn't quiet it, nor the penetration of my ass—it would fester until I took my last breath because as surely as Gage was a sadist, I was a reluctant slave with a nagging need to be my own damn person at least part of the time.

"I want to go back to the negotiation table."

"We're talking about your needs, not your wants."

I met his gaze with the glare of firm resolve. "I *need* to go back to the negotiation table."

His fingers slid into my hair, and he tugged my lips to his. "You had it right the first time, but for the duration of your pregnancy, we'll compromise. I don't expect things to stay the same while we navigate this."

"Thank you."

"But this habit you have of withholding shit? It ends now. Do you understand me?"

I nodded, blinking in quick succession to fight back the tears. "Yes, Master."

"My job is to help you carry these burdens, but I can't do that if you don't tell me what's bothering you."

I reached for his cheeks, and as we stood there, face-to-face, holding on to each other while we waited for the doctor to tell us everything would be okay, I finally found the words I needed to relay what my heart had been telling me for a year and a half.

"I need your permission to be imperfect. What if I'm too sick to take your cock in my mouth? What if I'm not in the mood for sex? And anal," I said with a gulp. "I don't want you to be disappointed if I...if I say no."

Dropping his hand to my chin, he ran his fingers along my jawline. "You're not allowed to say no to me, which makes your job simple. Trust me. I'll be careful with you, baby. Why can't you see that?"

"Because you hurt me."

"I've always hurt you, long before we married. Part of you even gets off on it, so this preoccupation of yours lately leaves me with one conclusion. You don't trust me enough to submit fully. You've given so much of yourself, but you're still holding on to the doubt in the back of your mind. It's an ugly voice in your head, and it'll do nothing but pick apart our relationship."

"I'll try harder, Master," I said, lowering my eyes.

A knock sounded, shattering our moment.

"We'll talk about this more later," Gage said as he moved away from me. The door opened slowly, revealing a petite woman in scrubs. The doctor introduced herself as Dr. Keenan, and her warm smile put me at ease instantly.

The appointment went as expected; first we went over our concerns about another tubal pregnancy, talked about our alternative lifestyle—Gage had found Dr. Keenan for a reason, as she wasn't quick to judge when it came to kink. Then came the degrading part. After changing into a gown, the doctor helped me fit my feet into stirrups and performed the exam. I kept my eyes on Gage the whole time, counting the seconds until she finished.

"I'd like to do an ultrasound," she said. "I believe you're further along than you thought."

"By how long? A few days?"

"More like a few weeks."

I pushed myself up on my elbows, and she held out a hand to help me into a sitting position. "But I had a period about…five weeks ago, I think."

She asked me a few more questions and mentioned something about implantation bleeding before readying the ultrasound machine. I reclined once more, and as Dr. Keenan squirted a jelly-like substance onto my flat belly, Gage moved to my side and took my hand, squeezing my fingers.

I kept my gaze glued to the monitor, but terror fisted my throat. What would we do if that machine trampled our dreams?

"Everything's going to be okay, baby," he said, his voice low yet full of certainty.

I grabbed onto his words and wrapped myself in them. I had to trust that he was right. Besides, if I were further along than I thought, then didn't that mean the truly nail-biting stage of my pregnancy had passed?

The doctor pressed the hand-held device to my belly and moved it around until she found the right spot. "There's your baby," she said with a smile. "My, hear that strong heartbeat."

Thump-thump, thump-thump, thump-thump…

"You're about ten weeks."

"Oh my God." Through my tears, I stared at the image of our tiny baby in awe. Tearing my gaze away long enough to meet Gage's eyes was so damn hard, but I wanted to see his reaction as much as I wanted to take in the black and white picture of the child growing inside me. Gage brought the back of my hand to his lips, his blue eyes bright with wonder, and that small gesture was nearly my undoing.

17. EDGY

"Eve!" I called out, thrusting my arms into the sleeves of a knee-length sweater. "Where's your jacket?"

"Um…I think I left it in the bathroom."

As I tied the sash around my waist, she ran down the hall, and I called after her to hurry up. "The bus is going to be here any second!"

She returned thirty seconds later, trying to shove her right arm through a sleeve that was partially inside out.

"Here, baby. Let me." Pulling the garment from her body, I tugged on the sleeves then helped her push her arms through. We rushed out the front door, and a misty rain fell, leaving tiny pin-sized drops of water in our hair and on our clothes.

"Did you get my Halloween costume yet?"

Shit.

"I'll get it tomorrow."

"Mom," she whined.

I sighed, ill-equipped to handle her mood swings this morning. I was barely able to keep up with my own, and it didn't help that what little breakfast I'd eaten sat lodged in my throat, just waiting to make an appearance.

"You'll love it, I promise." As soon as the bus pulled up, I bent and gave her a hug. "Have a great day at school."

"Bye, Mom!" She stomped up the stairs, and as the yellow bus started to wheel away, she waved at me from her seat at the front. I waved back, then I stood for a few minutes, eyes closed, face upturned toward the falling mist, and just breathed. The cool air soothed the nausea, and the serene chirping of birds, combined with the gentle rustle of leaves, eased the tension from my muscles.

I sensed Gage's presence before he touched me.

"What are you doing out here?" he asked, resting his hands on my shoulders.

"Fresh air helps the nausea."

Wrapping his arms around me, he rested his chin on my shoulder. "Then we'll stand out here as long as you need, though I'd hate for you to come down with a cold."

"Cold weather doesn't cause—"

"Illnesses, I know." He let out a soft laugh into my hair. "Viruses do."

"And bacteria."

"That too."

Standing in the rain with him like this gave me a sense of deja vu. He let me have my meditative moment for a couple minutes longer, then he tugged on my arm, and I followed him back into the house. The day held a weird sort of energy I couldn't put my finger on. The air was rife with it as we settled in at the dining table again, where we'd gathered for breakfast before Eve had to leave for school.

Gage folded his newspaper and set it aside, and the way he scrutinized me made me edgy. I crossed my arms, suddenly chilled despite my sweater. The ball was tonight, and he'd taken the day off from work so we could...talk.

"You should try finishing your breakfast," he said, nudging my partially eaten plate of pancakes toward me.

"I'm sorry. I'm just not hungry right now."

"Do you want me to fix you something else?"

"I don't know. Maybe in a while."

With a sigh, he grabbed my hand. "Are you nervous about tonight?"

Avoiding his gaze, I darted my tongue out and wet my lips. "Which part?"

"The latter half of the evening."

"Yes."

He leaned forward and brushed the hair from my eyes. "You have nothing to be scared of, baby. Just let go and trust me."

"I'm trying, but I still think we should go over a few things."

He settled back into his seat. "I was up most of the night considering everything you said yesterday at Dr. Keenan's office, and I came to a decision, Kayla." The tone of his voice put me on alert, and I sat up straighter.

"You said you needed security, so I'm going to give it to you in the only way I know how. There will be no negotiations. The only thing I want from you is trust. In return, I will give you a safe word after tonight."

"A safe word?"

"Yes."

Technically, I had a safe word, but I never used it, and he didn't allow me to use it during punishments. "In what way will this be different from what we do now?"

He cleared his throat. "You know how I dislike giving you control, but in this situation, a certain amount of it is necessary, so long as you don't abuse the privilege. Because that's what it is. A privilege. You're my slave, but you're also carrying my child, so I want you to feel... safe." Lowering his head, he ran his fingers through his hair, and I realized how difficult that concession had been for him to make.

"I do feel safe, Gage."

"Do you?" he asked, lifting his head.

"Yes."

"Even when I'm punishing your ass?"

I gulped. "Yes, Master." Didn't mean I liked or even handled his punishments well, but I hadn't truly feared him since...

Since the day I cheated on him with his brother.

"Then why are you having trouble submitting?"

That was a good question. Fear of the unknown, perhaps, or that voice inside me that constantly shouted how love shouldn't be like this. "I guess it's in my nature to dig my heels in."

"Baby, I love that part of you more than anything. But rules are rules, and you'll never be allowed to deny me." He paused, letting his statement sink in. "That being said, if something I'm doing is too difficult to handle, no matter how well-deserved, you have my permission to speak up about it."

"Kinda hard to speak up when you gag me half the time," I grumbled.

"I don't gag you to quiet your opinions. I do it when I need you to hear what I'm saying, without interruptions or distractions. And Kayla," he said, a gruff note entering his tone. "I do it because it turns me the fuck on."

God, how I loved turning him on.

"Are you still feeling ill?"

"No, Master." Why was my voice suddenly raspy? Tight with need and want? Had he conditioned my body's response to fall in tune with the way he spoke to me?

"Don't move," he said, scooting his chair across the hardwood. "I'll be right back." He gathered our dishes before disappearing into the kitchen. Running water sounded from the other room for a few seconds before he returned.

"Hop up here," he said, patting the middle of the dining table.

"Master?" My attention swerved between his face and his hand, which still rested on the table.

"I'm fairly certain you understood me. I want you up here now, legs spread. I intend to make you edge all day."

Just in time for tonight, so I'd be so out of my mind with wanting him that I wouldn't question the things he planned to do to me. Even as I slid onto the table in front of him, opening my legs and exposing myself to his darkening gaze, I knew his end game, and it would be one hell of a ride that would soar me to the highest of highs before dropping me into the bowels of agony.

He buried his face between my thighs, and that's how much of the day passed. Between bouts of morning sickness, Gage pushed me to within inches of tumbling over the forbidden ledge of ecstasy.

On the table, bent over his desk, in the shower, even against the window with the curtains drawn. That had been particularly fucked up, as he'd positioned me facing our street while he crouched between my legs, out of view. He'd licked me to madness underneath my skirt, and the only way to save my dignity had been to keep my face blank as the cars rolled past.

In the end, I'd failed. With my hands balled against the glass, I'd begged him to let me come, heedless of who might be watching my grand moment of weakness as my husband pushed his tongue into my pussy again and again.

Of course, he'd ignored my pleas. But at least there was one positive side effect to having been pushed to the edge all day; I throbbed for release so much that the nausea subsided, and I I figured I'd have no problem digging into dinner like a starving, ravenous pig.

After Leah's mom picked up Eve, and the evening fell into darkness, I entered the bedroom to prepare for the charity ball. That's when I noticed a box sitting on the end of the bed.

Gage hovered behind me, his body heat warming my back as excitement zinged through my veins. Damn, this man...his biggest achievement in life was turning me inside out and upside down. Tonight would challenge me, scare me, but knowing Gage, it would also make me stronger in my submission. Tonight would be the first true test of our roles since finding out about the baby.

"Are you curious what's inside?" he asked.

"Of course I am."

"Address me properly."

"I'm sorry, Master."

"Your pregnancy doesn't give you license to act like a brat, and it won't prevent me from punishing your hole." To drive home his point, he drew a finger between my butt cheeks, bottom to top. "Anal penetration won't harm the baby if done with care."

I wanted to argue, mostly because I hated when he punished my asshole, but the doctor had given us the rundown on what was safe and what wasn't. As long as my pregnancy continued on a normal, healthy path, Gage still had plenty of room to make me bend.

"May I open the box now, Master?"

"You may," he said with a playful swat to my bottom.

It was enough to send me into motion. I sensed him lingering a couple of feet behind me as I crossed to the bed. That box drew my attention like a beacon, with its gorgeous burgundy color, accented with black lace and trimmed in gold. I pried the top off and pushed the tissue paper aside to reveal black rope and a jeweled butt plug. Dread and longing collided inside me until I couldn't decide whether to run from what he had planned, or beg for it. I lifted the rope and turned to face him.

"I thought you could use a couple of accessories to

match your dress." His mouth curled into a smug smile.

"My dress?" I rubbed the silky rope between my fingers.

"Come," he said, holding out a hand.

Sliding my palm into his felt as natural as breathing. He led me to our wardrobe and unzipped a garment bag that hadn't been in there that morning when I'd dressed.

"Wow," I breathed, more than taken with the gown that spilled from the bag. The dress was the same deep burgundy as the butt plug, and the skirt was as full as a ballroom gown. I ran my fingers over the black and gold beadwork that adorned the front of the strapless corset-styled bodice.

"What a divine creation," he said, fingering the satin material, but his gaze never left me. "Wearing clothing should be illegal. If I could escort your naked body to this ball and get away with it, I would." A corner of his mouth tilted up. "I guess this dress will have to do, at least until we get to the better portion of the night."

The *after* party.

He freed the dress from the bag before escorting me back into the bedroom. I clutched the rope, which was long enough that the end trailed behind me on the hardwood floor. He carefully arranged the dress on the bed before moving toward me with purpose, one hand outstretched, palm up.

"Hand me the rope, please."

It slipped from my fingers, like silk pouring from my hand to his, and a chill broke out on my skin as I watched him fold it in half. I had no clue what he was about to do.

The upcoming night held many intrigues—beginning right here in our bedroom.

"Extend your arms."

As I stood with my arms spread and feet shoulder-width apart on the floor, he wound the rope above and below my breasts, his fingers grazing my skin in a way that caused gooseflesh. Then he drew the rope over my nipples—fuck, they were sensitive—and weaved it into neat little knots as he worked, before making a loop around my neck. Finally, he finished by running the rope between my legs. All of my most sensitive parts came alive under the restraining friction of the silky twine. I couldn't move without arousal flaring to life.

He halted in front of me, his eyes bright with mischief and lips curved in a knowing smirk as if to say how he'd be the one stroking me by proxy all night long.

"Bend over the bed," he said, grabbing the butt plug.

I found freedom in yielding to his commands, despite fighting myself daily on giving him my unconditional trust. The more I resisted, the more firm his resolve to exorcize my last thread of independence tonight. As he slipped the plug in, making my pussy shamefully wet from that single action alone, I thought he might just achieve his goal. I was tired of battling an internal war I'd never win.

"The plug is synced to my cell. For the duration of the night, when it vibrates, I expect you to touch yourself."

My breath caught in my throat. "Where? The women's restroom?" Damn it. He knew how I hated submitting in public places.

"No, that's too easy. An empty hallway or room will suffice. I want you in fear of getting caught."

I turned wide, frightened eyes on him. "Master, please!"

"Shh," he whispered, pressing a finger to my lips. "The ball is being held at the Davenport Estate. There are plenty of semi-private places to masturbate. I expect you to find one upon command, but you're not to bring yourself to orgasm." Running a palm down my ass, he pressed his lips to my neck. "This will help you get into the right mindset for our plans after the ball."

Plans that included other people. Oh, how I despised these plans, probably more than he'd ever know.

"It's getting late. Time to dress," he said, slapping my ass. He crossed to the bureau and produced two masks—one for him and one for me.

"What's a masquerade ball without a mask?"

18. BENEATH THE MASK

Gage pulled through the iron gates of the Davenport Estate, and as we approached the front of the traditional brick mansion, I marveled at the lush, sprawling lawns that seemed to reach the horizon. Rolling to a stop at the main entrance, he alighted and rounded the hood, warding off a well-meaning valet who moved to open my door. As Gage assisted me from the car, helping me maneuver the full skirt of my ballgown, I took in our surroundings. By no means did we live in anything other than the lap of luxury, but this place was on a whole other level of opulence.

Fitting my hand in the crook of his arm, Gage escorted me onto the stone walkway that led to the front door. A light breeze blew through my hair, and I brushed the strands from my face, my wide-eyed gaze riveted to the nearby pond. The night was mild, absent of even a drop of rain. Fluffy clouds parted, allowing the silver light of the crescent moon to ripple onto the pond. The moon seemed to hover—just a tiny dip and the bottom would touch the pond, breaking the glass-like surface.

A man in a tux greeted us at the door. He took our jackets before pointing us in the direction of the mansion's host. And speaking of tuxedos…good God, how I ached to rip off my husband's and have my way with him. I peeked at him from the corner of my eye, appreciating how his chest filled out the vest and overcoat. But he caught me ogling, and his eyes sparkled behind the black mask he wore.

"Mr. and Mrs. Channing. Welcome to our home," said a man who also knew how to wear a tux, though he lacked Gage's commanding presence, not to mention a pair of sexy indigo eyes and a cock I wanted to kneel for at this very moment.

Gage shook hands with the man as he introduced us.

"Nice to meet you," I said, failing to offer my hand because I knew the rules. No other man was to touch me, no matter the social etiquette. In the beginning, Gage had allowed that tiny concession, but not since I'd betrayed him with…

Better to not go there.

Mr. Davenport seemed unsurprised by my lack of manners, and something niggled in the back of my mind. Suddenly, I felt on display, naked despite wearing a gown heavier than seven layers of clothing.

"Pleased to meet you," our host said, and even though he didn't possess Gage's innate dominant manner, he had a head full of thick, blond hair and a broad smile that revealed the kind of perfect white teeth I'd seen in toothpaste commercials. "This is my wife, Virginia." He indicated the brunette holding onto his arm. Her hair was sleek and straight, and she had the kind of curvy waist I envied.

But her smile was as genuine as her husband's, and that was all that mattered. She stepped forward and gently took my arm. "How about we allow these men to do what men do at these shindigs? There are several ladies just dying to meet the woman who snatched the one and only Gage Channing."

Something about the way she spoke of Gage made me curious, and a little cautious. I shot him a quick glance, relaying so much with a furtive dart of my gaze.

May I go, Master?

With a slight nod, he bent and kissed my cheek. "Have fun, baby," he said, voice too intimate to be overheard. "Don't forget your task for the night."

I'd grown used to the butt plug. It wasn't overly big, so I didn't find it uncomfortable, and I certainly didn't miss the rectal burn the larger ones caused. Even so, now that Gage had reminded me of what I was to do, my ass suddenly felt too full—brimming with the promise of humiliation.

I swallowed hard as Virginia led me through the throng of people. Ballgowns of all colors brushed the parquet flooring, and men wore a variety of tuxedoes, from traditional black with long-tailed jackets to contemporary attire, embellished with colors from tasteful to…less tasteful.

She ushered me into another room where tables were grouped in strategic patterns around the dance floor. I instantly recognized the decor because I'd helped pick out the colors. Ironically, the ballroom matched my dress, and I wondered if that had been Gage's intention all along.

Probably so. Gage did everything by design.

"Over here," Virginia said, yanking on my hand and leading me to a table where four other women, also decked out in extravagant ballgowns, sat.

"Kayla," my hostess said, "I'd like you to meet…"

Too busy taking in the features of each woman, I tuned out their names, as I likely wouldn't remember them anyway. Not in this setting, with my heart pounding an irregular rhythm behind my breastbone.

The blonde with enviable curls and dark brown eyes nibbled on a crab-stuffed mushroom, her gaze shyly taking me in. The other three were all various shades of browns, but their hairstyles couldn't have been more different. One sported a cute pixie while the other two had longer lengths. The girl wearing a dress that could pass as a wedding gown wore her hair past her ass. The last of this brunette trio ran her fingers through layers that feathered around her flawless complexion.

These women were, in a word, gorgeous. And something about the way they interacted with each other —with ease and familiarity—told me their friendships had withstood the test of time. I sat with them for about forty-five minutes, nibbling on hors d'oeuvre and listening to their casual chatter.

But I felt disconnected, unable to relate to Blondie's endeavor to find the perfect piece of jewelry for her upcoming trip to Paris. Nor could I empathize with Pixie

Girl's indecision on which boarding school to send her daughter to next year.

Over my dead body would I send my children away.

Despite the world of differences between this group and myself, I still found their company pleasant, and I could see meeting up with them for lunch, or even a day of shopping if Gage allowed it.

Something told me he would. My gut chewed over this whole night in a way that frightened and excited me, and I sensed these women and their as yet named husbands were going to play a big part in our lives. Maybe Gage wanted us to have friends. The concept sounded kind of...nice.

I was lost in Virginia's talk about the next fundraiser she was in the process of organizing when the plug in my ass vibrated me out of my stupor. The telltale mechanical sound blazed my cheeks red, but no one seemed to hear it over the excited discussion of venues and caterers.

Rising from my chair, I excused myself to use the ladies room and headed in the direction that Virginia pointed out. But that wouldn't do. Gage had given me specific instructions, and they didn't involve hiding in a bathroom, safe behind a closed door.

Damn him.

A wall of French doors caught my eye to the right, and before I could give it more thought, I slipped outside and immediately wished I had my jacket. But the weather wasn't too bad, and doing Gage's bidding would be easier out here, where I had plenty of space to explore, between the stone walkways, spotted with benches and lanterns that invited people to meander through the gardens surrounding the gazebo.

Only a few stragglers braved the chilly night, but most of them kept close to the estate. Gage hadn't said a word about *not* going outside to touch myself, so I took off down the path, eyeing the shelter of trees that provided a backdrop for the gazebo. Ash trees were prominent throughout the grounds, and their autumn leaves—the color of burnt sienna and gold—quietly drifted to the grass like confetti at a party.

I found an unusually large tree a few feet from the gazebo, its trunk wide enough to conceal most of my body. And that's where I settled in for the duration of my first task, my back against the smooth bark as I gathered my gown up in the front and wedged my hand between my thighs, pushing Gage's rope to the side.

Oh God. The friction of that rope in the valley of my ass cheeks, and the way it pressed tight against my nipples amped me even hotter. Between the vibrations from the plug and the slickness of my needy pussy, left aching all day from Gage's denial games, I wasn't sure how I'd survive this.

But I had to, even if that meant visualizing spiders crawling all over me to keep from coming. Because I knew my husband well enough to know that he expected me to touch myself until the vibrations stopped.

It was all about control, and I'd better find some, or else.

But damn...

With a groan, I let my head fall back against the tree

and increased the circling motion of my fingers. And they were playing a dangerous game—touching in the perfect way with enough pressure to bring a massive rush of blood to my core.

So damn good. Could I get off and lie about it?

Not even an option. Not only would he know I was lying, but I'd break under my own guilt in two seconds flat. But shit…I was going to come. So close.

Too fucking close.

Growling, and more than a little angry, I banged my head against the trunk as I wrenched my fingers away from temptation. Just a few seconds, I promised myself, concentrating on breathing until my heartbeat slowed. But my ass still vibrated Gage's command, and I imagined his words as surely as if he'd spoken them into my ear.

Fingers in your drenched cunt, Kayla. Don't stop now.

Why did he have to torture me so damn much? I was never free of him—if his control didn't wrap me in metaphorical cellophane, then his voice echoed in my head, uttering filthy words that never failed to make me do his bidding.

Pushing my wet fingers back into the center of slick heat, I worked myself into a frenzy. My pussy throbbed with each stroke, and I climbed higher—so high I worried I'd float away, regardless of the consequences. Squeezing my eyes shut, I pleaded with a higher power to help me resist.

"Please, *please*…" My frantic whispers got lost in the breeze, drifting on the leaves, finding the kind of freedom I wasn't allowed. "Oh please…I *can't*…"

And that's when the vibrations stopped.

I wasn't sure how long I leaned against the tree, eyes closed, chest expanding and collapsing with each hard-won breath. Coming down took time—more time than I thought it would, considering I hadn't reached nirvana.

After a while, I started shivering, and I had just taken a step away from my hiding place when I heard voices. Pressing as flat as I could against the trunk, I prayed the cloak of darkness would conceal me to whoever had decided to encroach upon my private moment.

Two people stalled in front of the gazebo, and I recognized Gage immediately. The build of his shoulders, the way he walked, and the authority inherent in his tone —if nothing else gave him away behind his mask, those traits certainly did.

But he wasn't alone, and it took me an extra five seconds to realize the woman with him was Katherine. I pressed a fist to my mouth to cover a gasp.

"You've got five minutes before I have you thrown off the grounds," he said, and the undeniable anger in his voice leeched some of the tension from my body. This was not a rendezvous between two lovers on the down-low.

This was...I had no idea what this was, but forget the rules against eavesdropping; I wasn't about to blow my chance to find out more.

"Don't be so mean. No one's around, Gage. It's just us."

He closed the distance between them and grabbed her chin. "How pathetic are you? In what world would I want you here? You *weren't* invited."

A nearby lantern cast their faces in dim light, and I saw her full mouth curve into a sultry grin. "I can have anyone I want, Gage. It was child's play getting a date to this thing."

"Like I said," he growled, letting go of her chin in a move that bespoke of frustration. "Five minutes, Katherine. If you used our son to lure me out here—"

"You can't take her into the circle," she said, her voice rising in desperation. "It was supposed to be me!" She dropped to her knees and kissed his black dress shoes.

I chewed on my fist, swallowing vile hatred because the bitch was laying her nasty lips on what was mine. Those were my feet to kneel at. *My* shoes to kiss. I clenched my hands so tightly they cramped, but my gaze…I was transfixed, lost in the scene unfolding, like one would watch a horror film.

He stepped back, arms crossed, mouth in a scowl. "Get up. You're only embarrassing yourself."

"Please, Mr. Channing."

"Don't you dare 'Mr. Channing' me! She is my *wife*. When will you get that through your thick skull?"

Katherine lifted her head, but instead of the submissive pose I'd expected her to take—the one I adopted every fucking day—she sneered at him, her hands forming tight balls at her sides.

"Fine," she snapped. "She can be your wife all she wants. Little Miss Perfect with the adorable daughter and a penchant for scrubbing your house and serving your meals, but we both know you need more than that. I can give you what you need, baby."

"You never gave me what I needed. Why do you think I broke it off after a few months?"

His words blasted a hole in my heart, and I almost threw up on the spot. Rage simmered in my gut, heading for a full-on boil, and only closing my eyes and counting to ten kept the vomit at bay. He'd been fucking her.

For *months*.

I stepped forward, my thirst for a confrontation blazing an inferno in my veins, but he spoke before I exited the cover of shadows.

"Katherine, seriously, get up. What we had meant nothing. Hell, it was years ago. You need to move the fuck on."

"Like you were able to move on from her?"

"That's different."

"No, it's not, and I know you want me. Deep down, you know it's true. Why else would you have called me down to your basement?"

"That was about her. It had nothing to do with you." Leaning down, he grabbed a chunk of her hair. "I will not repeat myself. Get the *fuck* up."

She struggled to her feet, and he instantly let go of her. "After the shit you pulled last week, you're lucky I don't go after full custody. Your behavior makes me question how fit you are to be a mother to Conner."

She smirked at him. "You're just pissed because I forced your wife to face her past in that hotel room." Planting her hands on her hips, she cocked her head. "The photo I sent you was nothing. They were all over each other."

That was it. I stormed from my hiding spot, and her face stopped my out-of-control fist. She covered her cheek, eyes wide. In my periphery, I registered Gage's equally stunned silence, stowing that rare expression away in the dregs of my mind to process later.

"Thank you for that," I told Katherine, forcing my voice on an even keel. "With these damn pregnancy hormones, I never know when my fist might go flying." I held my right hand up and contracted my fingers. "The thing has a mind of its own sometimes."

Slowly, she dropped her hand, and I was way too fucking pleased to see red smarting across her skin. Her face wasn't so perfect anymore.

"Wh...what?" Her eyes grew wider if that were possible. Two blue pools of utter disbelief—though whether from the punch I'd landed or from my pregnancy announcement, I didn't know. And I didn't care.

Planting my fist in Katherine Mitchell's face had felt...way too satisfying.

She turned incredulous eyes on Gage. "Are you seriously going to let her assault the mother of your child?"

I stepped forward before he could answer, invading her space. "You're nothing but a lying bitch, jealous over what you can't have," I said, meeting her glare head-on. "You think you're a special snowflake because you gave birth to his child?"

Something ugly took over—maybe my own version of jealous and possessive woman—but I felt my lips curl into a nasty smile. "You keep forgetting one vital fact. You're just the baby mama. But me?" I lifted an elated brow. "I'm his wife *and* the mother of his unborn child, so I guess that makes me the winner here, sweetie."

She stumbled back, and only then did I realize that I'd inched forward with each verbal strike to the bullseye of her venomous core. I would have kept on pushing, refusing to back down until the bitch fell flat on her ass, but Gage grabbed my shoulders.

"Come on, Kayla. She's not worth it, and this stress isn't good for the baby."

I knew he was right, but hell, I wanted to keep going at her until not a trace of her claim on my husband remained.

"If you're not gone in five minutes," Gage told her, "I'll send security after you." He veered me in the direction of the estate, and I caught a glimpse of something dark passing over her face, settling into the depths of her eyes.

The promise of payback.

She might be down this round, but she fully intended to dig her claws into what was mine....one way or another. Beneath the mask of momentary defeat lived an irate woman who issued a silent challenge.

Game on.

19. RENDEZVOUS

"Why were you out here, Kayla?"

"Why were you?" I shot back. Once again, I tried to pull from his grasp, but he wouldn't allow it. He had my hand in the crook of his arm, the picture of a perfect gentlemen, but as he placed his palm over the back of my hand, I knew the true reason he held onto me.

Power and control. It was such a Gage type of move that I shouldn't have been surprised.

The lights from the mansion lit up the patio several feet in front of us, but Gage steered us toward a bench. As I settled into the seat, he removed his jacket and draped it over my shoulders before taking the spot next to me.

"Do not disrespect me, Kayla. Answer the question."

"I'm sorry, Master," I said, lowering my gaze to my twiddling thumbs. But I wasn't really sorry—a large part of me still seethed from my confrontation with that bitch. Adrenaline pumped through my veins too fast, and I took a deep breath to get a grip on my emotions.

151

"I came out here to touch myself." From the corner of my eye, I noted how his shoulders seemed to release some of his tension.

He let out a breath. "Of course you did." He shot me a sideways glance. "Did you come?"

"No, Master."

"But you got close?"

His line of questioning more than frustrated me. "Shouldn't we talk about Katherine?"

"You still don't trust me," he said, matter-of-factly. "But to answer your question, Kayla, I went for a walk with Katherine because she said she needed to talk about Conner."

I turned to face him and laced our fingers together. "I do trust you. That's not what this is about. I feel like…"

He squeezed my fingers, and that small gesture of encouragement gave me the strength to forge ahead.

"I guess I feel like there's something I'm missing, or not understanding. We've been married for over a year, but she just won't let go. You were with her for *months*, but that was years ago."

The instant the words left my mouth, I realized how ridiculous I sounded, considering my brief time with Ian years ago. Cheeks flaming, I lowered my gaze, ashamed that I'd let my jealousy and doubt cloud what was right in front of me. It was like a bulb flashing behind my eyes.

"I feel so stupid," I whispered.

He tilted my chin, refusing to let me hide. "You're not stupid, baby. You're mine, which makes me yours, and you have every right to get angry. She's overstepping, but it won't last forever. Eventually, she'll move on." His hold on me tightened. "She'll move on because she has *no choice*."

His assertion was layered in meaning. People always had a choice, but in Gage Channing's world, his decree was law, and he always got what he wanted. I wasn't sure he was right—not after I'd punched the bitch before throwing my pregnancy in her face.

"I'm only going to say one more thing about what went down back there," he said, nodding in the direction of the gazebo, where thankfully I found no sign of Katherine. "Because I won't allow her to ruin this night for us."

My breath stalled in my lungs as I waited for him to continue. Whatever he wanted to say, I sensed the importance.

"You were fucking amazing," he said, voice hoarse as he palmed my cheek. "If you're wondering why I didn't stand up for you, it's because I didn't have to. Watching you in action, with your claws bared and fighting for what's yours, was the best foreplay imaginable. I can *not* wait to get my hands on you tonight."

His words arrowed straight between my legs. "Master?" I breathed, fighting the urge to cover my suddenly aching nipples as visions of the two of us tore through my mind.

"What is it, baby?"

"I'm so wet." A whimper drifted from my lips, and I pressed my thighs together.

"Spread them," he ordered, a seductive timbre

holding his voice captive.

"But what if someone—"

"I don't care who's watching. Spread your legs." And he truly didn't give a fuck. His gaze remained on me, and he brought his hand to my cheek again, preventing me from searching our surroundings for bystanders.

Wetting my lips, I inched my thighs apart, horribly self-conscious as a hint of air drifted up my legs.

"If you don't spread your legs like you mean it, I will bend you over my lap and expose your ass."

Oh, fuck. That shouldn't make me so hot, but it did.

I spread wide open, and he slipped a warm hand underneath my full dress. He didn't bother easing into it —his fingers filled my pussy in a forceful thrust.

"Master," I groaned, arching my back.

"So fucking wet." He licked his lips. "Who owns this sexy-as-fuck cunt?"

"You do, Master." And he was driving me crazy because he refused to move his fingers. They'd laid claim to my drenched opening, and they seemed content to stay seated there as if my body was but a glove for those digits.

"Please," I practically sighed, falling into the deep sea of his eyes. No one else existed—it was just the two of us, nose-to-nose, his left palm on my cheek while his right hand drove me insane.

"You can beg all you want, but you're not coming."

"Why are you doing this to me?"

One corner of his mouth lifted. "Because I can." Leaning forward, he dipped his tongue between my parted lips. "Because I love to watch you come undone, nothing holding you back." He crooked his fingers inside me, and I moaned against his lips. "If I told you someone was watching us this very minute, would you still beg me to fuck you with my fingers?"

"Yes, Master." I kissed him, eyes fluttering shut, and spread my legs as wide as my tired muscles would allow. He tangled his tongue with mine for a few lust-filled seconds then pulled away.

"What if I wanted to lick your beautiful cunt while strangers watched? Would you beg me to do it?"

"*God*," I choked past the desire strangling my throat.

"I'm not your God, but I am your Master. Beg me, Kayla."

"I need you," I said with a whimper. "Fuck me, Master. I'm begging."

"Mmm," he murmured, scraping his teeth over the sensitive part of my neck, "your cunt is begging. Know the difference, baby."

"It needs you. Bad."

"Yes, it does. But your belly is growling, so your cunt will have to wait." He rose to his feet, and it was a good thing he pulled me to mine because I knew my legs would have folded without his support.

He led me back inside in time for the first course of an elaborate meal, and I wondered if everyone could guess at the mess between my legs with one glance at my flushed face. My lust for Gage consumed me, and I was certain I gave off whore-like pheromones that no mask in the world could disguise.

20. A TEST OF TRUST

I made it through dinner and dessert in a daze, politely nodding upon what I hoped were the right cues, and speaking only when directly spoken to. But my mind had zeroed in on the hot need between my thighs. Gage had mastered the art of controlling me through denial, and when he played with my head like this, I might as well be a puppet dangling on the other end of his strings.

Sometime later, long after we'd eaten our last course, he dragged my reluctant feet to the middle of the dance floor. Couples crowded around us from all sides—at least that's what it felt like despite the cathedral ceiling over the spacious ballroom. My husband's unyielding finger titled my chin in his direction, demanding my undivided attention. He pressed a hand to the small of my back and brought me into his arms. We swayed to the music, lost in our own world, mindless of the time passing. I could dance like this with him forever, one cheek nestled against his chest, moving more to the sound of his heartbeat than to the music.

"It's time," Gage whispered into my ear.

He might as well have poured ice water over my head. I withdrew from the circle of his arms, and only then did I notice how the guests had mostly disappeared. Hired help in crisp black and white uniforms began clearing tables.

Wordlessly, Gage ushered me from the ballroom. We headed toward a grand staircase with ornately carved wooden banisters, but instead of climbing to the second or even third floor of the estate, he steered me to the left of the stairs where we disappeared through an archway.

"Where are we going?"

Instead of answering, he laced our fingers together and escorted me halfway down a long corridor before opening another door and urging me into what appeared to be the library, going by the floor-to-ceiling shelves housing books. Some of them were old and worn, possibly antiques. The room offered privacy in a claustrophobic nature, as not a single window allowed a beam of light from the moon or a ray of warmth from the sun during the day.

Even though he'd removed his mask, I recognized Mr. Davenport instantly. He sat in a chair in front of the fireplace, his lean body nestled in dark brown leather. "It's an honor to have the two of you join us tonight," he said, his smile reaching his eyes.

I turned to Gage for instruction because I was way out of my element here. I didn't know what to expect or what was expected of me.

"My wife is in the dark about all of this, so please

forgive her lack of protocol. She'll know better after tonight."

Our host narrowed his thick brows. "Do you need a few minutes to discuss it with her before we get to the nondisclosure?"

"Thank you, but that won't be necessary. This is a lesson of trust for her."

"I see," the other man said, nodding. "Please, make yourself comfortable, Channing." He gestured to another chair to the right of him. A crystal decanter sat on a table alongside two tumblers.

Gage led me to where the other man sat and pointed at the floor in front of the table. "You may kneel here."

"Yes, Master." Regardless of our audience, the title slipped off my lips, as natural as breathing, and I sank to my knees, arranging my dress over a plush Persian rug as I did so.

Gage poured two fingers then settled into the high back armchair.

Mr. Davenport laid a document and pen down on the table. "It's standard, but feel free to read through it."

Burning with curiosity, I watched Gage go over the paper, certain his astute gaze left not a single word unread. With no hesitation, he signed his name at the bottom before passing the pen to me.

"You need to sign as well. It's just a standard nondisclosure agreement. You're not allowed to speak to anyone about what goes on during these sessions."

Sessions…as in plural. I tried not to gulp as I pushed upward, standing on my knees so I could reach the paper.

"Welcome to our circle," Mr. Davenport said. "I must admit to being pleasantly surprised you finally took me up on my invitation," he told Gage.

My husband merely shrugged. "I guess I was waiting for Kayla." He leaned forward and brushed his fingers under my chin. "And she wasn't quite ready until now."

The other man rose. "Wonderful. You'll find a robe for your slave at the top of the stairs. We require that new slaves disrobe in front of everyone their first time in the circle."

I felt my jaw slacken, but I didn't dare look at Gage. If I did, I might beg for him to take me home.

"If that's all then," Mr. Davenport stated rather than asked, "we'll see you down there in a few minutes." He gathered the document and crossed to the wall of shelves before pulling out a book. Much to my astonishment, two bookcases wheeled outward and to the sides, revealing a secret staircase.

"Is this some sort of secret society?" I asked after those stairs seemed to swallow our host.

"In a way, yes." Gage stood and held out a palm, assisting me to my feet. "Let's get this dress off."

I shrank back, fists crossing over my breasts. "I want to go home."

Gage frowned. "Now is not the time for you to rebel, baby. I've waited years for this. You're the only woman I've ever wanted to take into the circle."

"Why me?" It was a stupid question, and a desperate one I'd thrown out to stall him.

"Address me properly."

"I'm sorry, Master." Sorry wasn't even close—my mind spun in all directions, trying to latch on to something that made sense. How had we gone from Master and slave in the privacy of our home to this?

"When spoken to by the men in the circle, you'll address them as *Sir*, myself excluded. I'm your Master, and you'll address me as such." He straightened his spine, rising high over my quivering form. I stood on my feet in front of him, but my will was but a tiny ball of nothing, cowering on the floor.

"As for the other slaves," he continued, "you won't speak to them unless directed to." Carefully, he removed my mask and set it on the table before taking his off as well. But as he reached for me, I stepped out of line again.

"Please don't make me do this, Master."

"Do you trust me?"

"Yes, Master." But wanting to trust someone and doing so were two different things.

"Then prove it," he said. "Obey me. I promise you won't be touched by anyone but me."

No, I'd just be used and humiliated in front of his societal bigwig friends. Allowing him to unzip my dress took more self-control than I thought I possessed. As that zipper slid down my back, I clenched my fists and mashed my lips together. Why did the idea of submitting to him in front of others seem so daunting? Compared to what he put me through daily, having an audience shouldn't bother me so much.

My dress fell in a heavy pile on the floor, surrounding

my shaking limbs with the finest fabric money could buy. Gripping his offered hand, I worked my heels off before stepping outside the circle of discarded formalwear, and goose pimples erupted on my skin as he slowly freed my body from his rope binding.

"Are you ready?" he asked, folding the silky twine before pocketing it.

Not even close, but I'd be damned if I allowed this night to be the catalyst for a breakdown.

"As ready as I'll ever be, Master."

Gage herded me to the top of the stairs, where the "robe" hung on a hook. Robe, my ass. The garment was nothing more than a sheer peignoir.

"Whether you receive pain or pleasure tonight is up to you," he said, holding the lingerie open so I could push my arms through the long, flowing sleeves. Impossibly, I felt more exposed with it on.

"How so, Master?"

"If you behave, you won't be punished."

"That doesn't reassure me, Master."

"Why not?"

"Because you love my pain." Promises or not, he'd find creative ways to make me stumble.

Taking my chin between two commanding fingers, he pressed his lips to mine for a fleeting moment. "You know me so well."

The winding staircase took us to a room hidden below where the ball had been held. My skin chilled from the cold, or maybe from nerves. A door came into view, and Gage halted.

"You will follow my directions and only mine. Do you understand?"

"Y-yes, Master." I swallowed hard, but nausea busted through my resolve. "Can I have a safe word?"

"You don't need a safe word. You asked why you? This is why. You give me what I crave most. You give me the honor of truly owning you. Trust that I know what you can and can't handle."

Oh God. I was close to panicking.

"No gags," I begged.

He ran a thumb across my lips. "Considering your condition, I wouldn't have gagged you anyway. This is what I'm talking about, Kayla. You don't trust me to take care of you." Sharp disappointment drew his face taunt, deepening his indigo eyes.

"I'm sorry, Master." My failure at pleasing him sucked the strength from me, and my knees gave out. Wrapping my arms around his legs, I nestled my cheek against the smooth fabric of his pants. "I want to make you proud."

"You're making me hard."

Those words had the power to flip that mysterious switch inside me. From despair to arousal in less time than it took to inhale. Gazing up at him, I exhaled my reservations and grabbed his offered hand.

He propelled me to my feet, and though my body still shook from fear of the unknown, I felt stronger at my core as he wedged open that door and ushered me toward the next test of my submission.

21. THE CIRCLE

The sweet aroma of cigars drifted through the space that could only be described as elaborate...or decadently sensual from the candlelight that washed the room in a soft glow. This was not a basement, but a huge circle of a room, and Gage and I stood at the edge. Directly in the center sat a group of people, unsurprisingly in a circle. The men relaxed in chairs, their formal attire in various stages of undress as they talked, drank, and smoked. The five women I'd met earlier in the evening kneeled at their feet, sans their masks.

Blondie was completely naked, and her husband had gagged her mouth. Tears lingered on her long lashes, and I wondered what she'd done to earn the punishment of silence. To their left, Mr. Davenport puffed on a cigar, his legs spread to accommodate his wife's bobbing head. He helped her along, his fingers sifting through her sleek hair. He downright petted her as she sucked him with lazy strokes of her slurping mouth.

The other three women kneeled like Blondie, only

none of them were entirely naked. The girl who'd worn a white gown earlier now sported thigh-highs and nothing else. Pixie Girl was trussed up in shibari that concealed her private areas in the intricate design. The rope wound around her breasts, torso, and limbs in gorgeous weaving. She was bound to the spot, unable to rise to her feet with the way her arms and had been tied behind her, wrists connected to ankles.

The fifth woman wore only nipple clamps, and I resisted the urge to cover my breasts at the sight. Clenching the chain between her teeth, she tensed her jaw as she struggled to pull on the clamps. I watched her in morbid curiosity, wondering if she wanted the extra pain that pulling on that chain caused, or if she was yanking on it because the alternative would be worse. What would happen if she let it slip from her mouth?

I wasn't sure I wanted to know.

This place set me on edge, and not because it was home to displays of painful implements or torture stockades. Rather, the understated deviance in the room unsettled me to the bone.

Gage tugged on my hand, and as I followed him to the circle, I couldn't take my eyes off the two beds situated opposite each other across the room, with their canopies draped in gossamer gold. Those beds weren't made for privacy; they'd been set up as a stage for fucking, sitting high atop platforms that necessitated a five stair climb just to reach them. Love seats and chairs surrounded each platform, inviting the remaining couples to watch...or join in on the fun.

My stomach wanted to take a dive at that disturbing realization, but all I had to do was remind myself of Gage's possessiveness, and the fact that he'd promised no one but him would touch me.

"Welcome to the circle," the men chorused in sync as if they'd rehearsed that greeting.

Mr. Davenport, regardless of having his wife's mouth wrapped around his cock, leaned forward slightly. "The floor is yours," he told Gage.

"Thank you." Gage came to a stop and gently pushed on my shoulders, telling me without words to kneel.

My body obeyed, practically on auto-pilot, and the position put me at eye level with his hard-on. God, how I wanted to unzip him and take a page from Virginia Davenport's book. The woman's escalating moans as she feasted on her husband's cock did funny things to my insides.

"I need to go over one important ground rule," Gage said, his voice echoing through the room for all to hear. He grabbed my hair as if to ready me for a good mouth-fucking. "No one touches what's mine."

"Understood," someone said.

With a nod, Gage let me go. "It's time to disrobe," he said as my hair slid through his fingers.

I trudged to the center, watching as Gage settled into the only available seat in the circle, and slowly brought my hands to the front of the peignoir. The sheer fabric grazed my nipples, making my cheeks flush with awareness, and as I opened the material I imagined his mouth nipping at my breasts. I nearly moaned at the thought as the garment slipped from my shoulders and drifted to the hardwood under my bare feet.

"Good girl. Now turn around so everyone can see what's mine."

I made a slow circle, taking in the features of the men more closely than before. And while their eyes were on my erect nipples, I cataloged each couple. Blondie's husband was on the husky side, his shirt unbuttoned and pants undone. Pixie's man was as tall as Gage. His red hair was his most arresting feature; it was on the longer side, unruly and entirely sexy. The remaining men had classic dark good looks, but I found nothing interesting or special about them.

"Kayla?"

"Yes, Master?" I said, whirling back to Gage.

"Crawl to me."

And here came the real test. As soon as I got down on all fours, everyone would see how wet I was between my thighs. I wasn't sure why, but I found revealing my arousal more distressing than stripping in front of these people. I had no authority over the nakedness of my body, but my drenched pussy...I wished to be able to control that more than anything.

As I made my way across the floor to where Gage waited, I sensed five pairs of eyes on my ass—possibly even more if the women watched as well. He pulled the rope from his pocket and looped it through the discreet ring in my infinity collar, effectively leashing me with the rope I'd worn on my body all evening.

"Unzip me," he commanded.

That's when I hesitated, and not because I fretted over what he planned to do with me, but hell…I didn't want those women ogling my husband's cock. Fierce possessiveness rose in me, pumping blood through my system in pulsing bursts.

How could he stand those men's eyes on me? Especially with how jealous and possessive he was?

"Do I need to spank you?"

"No, Master," I said, reaching for his pants and freeing the button. As I pulled down his zipper, it dawned on me why Gage wasn't bothered by the prying eyes of other men. He was in control here, and they could look until their eyes fell out of their heads, but they couldn't touch.

The same could be said for the women. Mine, I mentally chanted as I parted his pants and revealed his cock, beaming with pride that I could call it mine. No other woman would come near it again. They'd have to get past my flying fist first. I balled my hands, darting my tongue over my lips to wet them as I gawked at my husband's impressive erection.

"Do you want me in your mouth?" He lifted his head, a sparkle in his gaze. "Davenport's slave seems to be enjoying the task."

I couldn't see the other couple, but I heard him chuckle over his wife's moaning.

"Yes, Master." The need to please him clawed at my composure. He had me too worked up, too wet at the epicenter of my depraved core. He'd managed to break me down like this in a mere day—to this desperate *thing* that would strip in front of strangers and beg to suck his cock.

Gage was a fucking sorcerer. I could come up with no other explanation.

"Baby, what if I don't want my cock in your mouth right now?" He withdrew a travel-sized packet of lube. "What if I want it someplace else?"

Cringing, I grabbed his knees for support. "As you w-wish, Master."

"Kayla," he murmured, tilting my chin up, "stand up and grab your ankles."

I pushed off his knees and stood on gelatinous limbs, and as I turned around to do his bidding, I found the others watching with appreciation and desire in their eyes. They were getting off on this voyeuristic showcase. Would watching these men dominate their wives get Gage hot and bothered as well? Would witnessing such sinful behavior get *me* off?

Listening to Virginia's moans had hit my bullseye, but only because I'd envied her at that moment. Fuck, I still did, considering that packet of lube and what it was obviously intended for.

I bent and grasped my ankles, and blood rushed to my head as Gage inched out the dry plug. He took extra time with the removal, being careful not to hurt me upon the toy's exit. Then I heard him tear into that packet, and between my spread thighs, I watched him lube his cock.

"You're going to sit your pretty ass onto my cock while we watch the show." He grabbed my hips and yanked me toward his lap, and I planted my hands on my knees to steady me. I tensed, body already fighting the intrusion of his shaft inside my tight hole, but he didn't bring me down onto him like I thought he would.

Quick and brutal, and powerless to stop him.

"Take me in as slow as you need to," he instructed, shocking me with his unexpected gift of control.

Holding onto the arms of the chair, I pressed onto his cock and willed my body to stretch around the intrusion. Minutes passed as I carefully worked him inside my ass, my knuckles going white even as I relaxed the muscles below my waist. Accepting his length and girth into my backdoor was a tall order, but I wasn't there yet, so I thrust downward and impaled myself fully. A gasp stalled in my lungs, and I held my breath for a few moments until I grew accustomed to the fullness in my ass.

"So good," he groaned into my ear. "Just sit like this for a while and watch."

His tone had a drugging effect on me. Or maybe it was his cock laying claim to my ass, but my belly heated, and my head spun with disorienting wooziness. Lifting heavy lids, I watched the going-ons happening inside the circle of this lair in a fog-like state.

Pixie had been released from her restraints, and now she sat on her husband's lap and rode him, her hips lowering her onto his cock over and over again.

Mr. Davenport yanked his wife's head up with an uncompromising fist in her hair.

"You haven't earned the privilege of getting me off yet."

She whimpered her disappointment.

"You're out of line, slave." His harsh voice stunned me, as did the way he addressed her. "You don't decide when I come down your throat. I do." Without further discussion, he pulled her head back into his lap and returned to sipping his drink.

The man to his left laughed, and they resumed their quiet conversation about stocks or some other crap I had no interest in listening to.

My attention veered to Blondie again, who'd switched positions with her husband. She reclined in the seat with her legs bent and feet on the chair's arms, knees spread wide. Her man stood before her, rubbing his chin as he watched her touch herself. His right arm dangled at his side, hand clenching a belt.

And now I understood why he'd gagged her. Even with her mouth full of rubber, her shrieks bounced off the walls. How the fuck did she manage to make so much noise behind that gag?

He brought his belt down on the rapid movement of her fingers. "No orgasms!" he hollered. "You took it without asking, and now you need to pay. Isn't that right?"

She nodded, but her whine indicated she felt differently about her husband's methods of punishing her. Just as Blondie's Master ordered her to touch herself again, Gage yanked on the rope attached to my collar. "Close your eyes," he said. "I want you to feel only me right now. They can watch all they want, but you'll feel and listen to only me."

"Yes, Master." My words were but a whisper, my body but a vessel for Gage to own. He pulled my head back until I reclined against his chest.

"Touch yourself," he said, placing his hands on my hips and lifting. As I buried my fingers between my thighs, he moved me up and down the entire length of his cock, sliding in and out of my ass with surprising ease.

And he was launching me to new heights, to the realm of ecstasy he'd teased me with all day.

My fingers practically spasmed over my clit. "Can I come, Master?"

"I haven't decided yet. Tell me how good my cock feels in your ass." He pushed in again, drawing a long shuddering moan from between tight lips.

"So fucking good, Master. Please let me come."

"Does it bother you that everyone here knows what a dirty girl you are?"

"No," I breathed, ten seconds away from exploding. Nothing mattered except the friction between our bodies and the trust flowing between our hearts.

Gage nipped at my earlobe, and his voice dipped low so only I could hear him. "You've made me so damn proud. Baby, come for me."

I'd never heard sweeter words.

22. KATHERINE'S WEB

The circle changed us, or maybe it only changed me. I'd found the experience empowering. Accepting Gage's dominion in the trenches of the Davenport Estate, while ten other people watched, had not only been kinky as hell but liberating. That night bound us together more tightly than the day we'd said "I do" in front of hundreds of people. It was magical how my doubts faded to nothing, almost as if they hadn't existed in the first place.

But insecurities have a way of camouflaging themselves in the absence of trials, and life threw me a mean curveball the day before Thanksgiving. As I pulled out a pumpkin pie from the oven, I heard the front door burst open before banging against the wall. Tossing the pot holders onto the counter, I wondered if Gage had come home early. Eve had gone to Seattle to visit her paternal grandparents for the holiday, so I knew she hadn't made the ruckus, though she'd normally get off the bus at this time.

I rushed from the kitchen and slid to a quick stop

upon the sight of Katherine seething in the foyer. "What the hell do you think you're doing?" I shouted, planting my hands on my hips. "Get out of my house."

"This is *your* fault," she said, taking a menacing step toward me. "You've done nothing but ruin my life since the day Gage set eyes on you."

I held my ground, refusing to give her an inch, especially in my own home. "Are you on drugs or something?" She didn't appear to be under the influence of anything other than pure hatred, but the unmistakable odor of whiskey assaulted my nose, and I gave that assessment a second glance.

She backed me into a wall before I saw it coming, and that's when I got scared. For all the things Gage had done to me, this was the first time in over a year that someone managed to transport me back to the days of my first marriage, when Rick had lost his temper while drunk off whatever bottle he'd gotten his hands onto for the day.

"Katherine, what are you doing?" My voice shook with the fear I couldn't hide, and I despised myself for the weakness.

"If he thinks he can fuck with my child, he's wrong."

"I-I don't know what you're—"

"Of course you don't," she spat. "Anything to protect the little wife. He wouldn't dare subject you to an unpleasant court battle."

Oh. The court date had arrived. Maybe it was due to pregnancy brain or preoccupation with the upcoming holiday, but I'd forgotten today was the day Gage had court over Conner's parenting plan.

"If you cared about your son at all, you wouldn't try to interfere with visitation."

"Visitation?" she shouted, pounding the wall to the left of my head. I closed my eyes, body tensing as my heart thundered in my chest. "He's going for full custody," she said, breath hot on my face. "Look at me, you bitch!"

Jumping, I opened my eyes, but I was frozen to the spot. I'd never seen her so unhinged. She'd always had a nasty, catty way about her when it came to me, but this was the woman who'd had my daughter over for play dates because Gage had demanded it.

This was the psycho he'd entrusted Eve with when he'd kidnapped me from my own bed in Texas. Letting my mind go back there for even a moment made me question my mental health because I'd married him.

And right then I wanted to strangle him for allowing Eve anywhere near this woman, not to mention for putting me in the position of needing to defend myself against her now.

"Get the fuck away from me." I shoved her, and she stumbled back a couple of steps. "I have no idea what you're talking about. Full custody?" Last I'd heard, he'd only wanted visitation.

Katherine gave a snide arch of her brow. "Didn't he tell you? Obviously, you convinced him I'm not fit to be a parent."

"You're giving me too much credit. You did that all on your own."

Her laughter grated, like a screeching cat at midnight,

or the squeal of a braking train. "Wow, you really are dense. Things were fine before you came along. But he traded his old obsession for a new one, so I guess that leaves me in the dust."

"What are you babbling about now?"

"I'm talking about Liz and Ian."

My eyes widened, and she laughed again.

"You know exactly what I'm talking about, don't you? But I'd bet money he didn't give you the really juicy details." She folded her arms. "Well, he wants to play hardball? He's got it. I bet he didn't tell you how Liz and I were besties in high school, or how he turned to me for comfort after she died."

"You're lying."

I knew she wasn't. Her words impacted me in the gut, stinking to fucking high heaven of truth—the sort I didn't want to face. I tried clinging to a mask of *I don't believe you, bitch*…but tears of betrayal dripped down my cheeks, giving me away. I swiped at them, angry at myself for letting her witness yet another episode of me falling short when it came to trusting Gage.

"He told me everything I need to know about you," I insisted, my words little more than a script my heart wished were true. "He was only involved with you for a few months."

"Oh my God—" She cut off and doubled over, laughing and laughing and laughing some more. "You're so fucking naive. Is that what he told you? A few months? We've been wrapped around each other for over a decade." Her expression sobered, and she straightened until she stood taller than my average height. "But then you came along, and suddenly I couldn't even get him to fuck me anymore. It's like he let go of a decade-long grudge to marry Susie-Fucking-Homemaker. How the fuck did you get him to do that?"

Maybe I *was* naive because I should tell her to leave, and threaten to call the police if she refused. But she'd obviously been drinking, and in my experience, people had loose lips when inebriated. They also tended to be dangerous, but I squashed the warning that buzzed through my head before it had a chance to take flight.

"Enlighten me then. Since I'm so naive as to believe what my husband tells me," I said, experiencing a small thrill at how her lips flattened upon my use of the word *husband*, "then why don't you set me straight?"

"You have no idea how happy I am to knock you off your high horse finally." She pushed past me and headed toward the kitchen. "Pour me a fucking drink, and I'll talk about Gage'a sordid past all you want."

This was a bad idea. She'd barged into my home and put her hands on me, and I wasn't stupid enough to believe for a moment that she was trustworthy.

But I was powerless to turn back now. Unlike the first time she'd duped me—when my instincts had screamed that she was lying—this time they hummed. Something was different about Katherine. She was a woman at the end of her rope, all hope lost with nothing to lose, and a woman like Katherine…she didn't go down without dragging someone else with her.

She knew things about Gage. Things I wished more

than anything he'd tell me, but I knew he never would. Despite his grandstanding about coming to him with my concerns or questions, he remained closed-off to discussions of the past.

For someone who lived to inflict pain, he sure avoided the emotional kind at all cost.

I pulled down a bottle of rum and poured a small amount into a glass before adding cola. She'd taken a seat at the bar, so I leaned against the opposite side, feeling safer with the counter between us. But the position also put me at an advantage. While she cast her attention on the drink between her manicured hands, I carefully slid my cell off the countertop and hit the record button. After what happened the last time we'd spoken alone, I wasn't taking any chances. If the bitch said or did anything wrong, I'd have it on audio.

"Start talking."

23. DEUCE IMPETUOUS

I will not fucking cry.

"Damn it," I muttered as a tear escaped. Gritting my teeth, I blinked rapidly and stuffed more clothing into the overflowing suitcase. An absurd amount of dresses rose above the rim, and as I shoved the pile down, I wished like hell I had some pants. Or even a few pairs of sweats. Definitely some underwear. But those finer things in life weren't allowed—not when it meant blocking my husband's access to his favorite place between my thighs.

I wrestled with the zipper, adding my body weight to the top of the case, and finally zipped it shut. If I walked out that door, I'd have nothing but what lay in a tossed mess inside. The remainder of my clothing filled the shelves, drawers, and hangers inside the walk-in wardrobe I shared with Gage.

Oh, God…Eve.

How was I supposed to tell her? She'd miss her bedroom, her toys. She'd miss *him.*

The reality of what I was doing hit me, and in a fit of

anger, I dragged the suitcase off the bed and kicked the damned thing until it fell over on its side. Okay, so I wasn't exactly thinking logically, but didn't a pregnant woman have the right to a meltdown after finding out her husband was nothing but a lying—

Don't go there.

But I went there anyway, torturing myself with every word the bitch had spoken. Nearly doubling over at the thought, I pressed a desperate fist to my lips and stifled a sob; sucked in quick breaths before letting them out in hot spurts that dampened my knuckles. Where had the tears come from? I'd promised myself I wouldn't cry anymore.

Pull it together, Kayla.

He was due to arrive in the driveway any minute now. Simone had begged me to leave before he got home, but if I were going to do this, I had to confront him first. Otherwise, he would never let me go. A hand dropped onto my shoulder, warm with comforting support. Simone didn't say a word, but she didn't need to. I knew she wouldn't leave my side, and that's why I'd called her. She was my safety net, the one person who wouldn't hesitate to hand Gage his ass if he tried railroading me. She was here to make sure I got out.

"You don't owe him anything," she said.

Nodding, I wiped my eyes. "I know."

I didn't know shit. My husband was the fucking devil incarnate, but he loved me. Didn't he? Or had it all been a lie? That was the problem—I didn't know anymore. My emotions had me trapped in the eye of a typhoon named

Gage Channing.

Simone's hand slid from my shoulder as I rebuilt my emotional fortress. I stood to the side in bitter numbness while she hauled my suitcase upright. She headed toward the bedroom door, rollers sounding on the hardwood behind her.

"It's okay to need some space, you know. If he loves you, he'll understand."

Folding my arms, I sank onto the end of the mattress. This particular spot bled with memories. He'd bend me over in a heartbeat and blast some sense into my ass if I let him. I couldn't let him get that close, or I'd crack wide open. Hell, I'd probably fracture regardless.

"I need to do this," I said, shaking my head just as his car sounded. "I need some space, but I also need…"

Answers.

Simone lingered by the bedroom door, chewing her bottom lip. Uncertainty was a strange feature on her face. She didn't do uncertain—she was a pick-a-path-and-follow-it kind of woman.

"I'll be okay, Simone. I promise."

She let out a sigh. "I'll be right out there," she said, jabbing a finger in the direction of the living room. She left the door cracked open upon her exit, and her absence echoed in my ears. The room hummed a solitary tune, and each lonesome note poked at my will. But a single question repeated on loop within the chaos of my foggy mind. Could I really go through with this?

I had no time to mull over the question, or to second-guess my knee-jerk reaction to what Katherine had told me. The front door opened and closed, and I heard murmuring in the living room, then footsteps. Firm, urgent steps that brought him down the hall. I withdrew my cell from my coat pocket and gripped it in a sweaty hand. He shoved the door open, and my pulse skyrocketed.

Gage took one look at my red eyes and splotchy face, and his complexion blanched.

"Are you okay?" He covered the distance in a few long strides, but I held up a hand.

"Please don't touch me."

He halted a couple of feet in front of me. "What's going on? Tell me you're okay."

"Physically, I'm fine." I rose, tilting my chin up, and met his eyes. "Katherine pushed me against the wall, but that was the extent of it."

A vengeful storm brewed in his gaze, and he clenched his hands at his sides. I wondered what his reaction would be after he heard every detail of his sordid history from Katherine's own mouth, courtesy of the recording the bitch knew nothing about.

"What did she do?" he asked, his voice ominous enough that I shivered.

"She told me all the things you wouldn't." I handed him my cell, screen displaying the play button.

He glanced at the phone, brows furrowing in confusion. "Kayla, you'd better start explaining right now."

"Press play. I'd rather let Katherine explain since she's so good at it." I edged around his body and stood a few feet away.

His thumb moved over the screen, and as Katherine's voice infiltrated our private space, some of her words slurring a bit, Gage captured me in his gaze. For twenty minutes we listened to the foundation of our marriage fissure at our feet, all the while looking at each other as if the other could save us from the wreckage.

He shut the recording off. "I've heard enough."

"No," I said, gesturing to the phone. "You haven't gotten to the best part. She threatened our baby." I settled a hand over my belly, seething at her parting shot. "The bitch actually looked at my stomach and threatened to hurt me if you take Conner from her."

His face twisted into something ugly, and he launched the phone through the open door where it thumped against a family portrait in the hall before dropping to the hardwood. I probably had a cracked screen now, if the cell still worked at all. A few seconds later, Simone appeared in the doorway.

"Kayla?"

"I'm okay. I'll be out in a minute."

Gage thrust an irate finger in her direction. "She's not going anywhere with you."

Simone wasn't someone Gage could command, and she made that clear by the way she planted a hand on her hip. "Good thing she has a brain of her own and two feet to carry her out of this house."

"Simone, please. I'm okay."

"And there's this little thing called the Portland PD," she added. "So if you think of laying a hand—"

"What I do with my hands is none of your business, and neither is this conversation." He stalked toward her, and his expression must have been fierce because Simone backed into the hall. "Get the fuck out of my house before *I* call the police to have you removed for trespassing." Indignation arched her brows as Gage slammed the door in her face. He turned the lock then crossed to me, and he wasn't stopping this time.

"Gage, no—"

"It's Master."

"Fuck you!" I spat as he lifted me and tossed me over his shoulder. "A real Master wouldn't hide an engagement. You lied to me!"

"I didn't lie to you." He set me on my feet in front of the spanking chair.

"What do you call it then?"

"I call it fucking history." Settling into the seat, he pulled me over his knees.

"You said you fucked her for a few months. Ha! You've known her since high school. She was Liz's best friend, for fuck's sake."

"It's in the past, Kayla. It was history the instant I—"

"Had me in your sights as the ultimate plan for revenge?" I scowled at him. "I can see why you fucked her now—anything to further your quest against the bitch that betrayed you!"

He yanked up my skirt. "Have you told me every little detail about your past with my brother?" He ended the question with a smarting strike to my ass.

"No!" I anticipated the painful intrusion of his

thumb, but a yelp still escaped.

"Honest to fuck, baby, I don't want all the details. Do you think I want to know how he fucked you? I know you loved him, and that's hard enough to swallow." Another slap landed on my ass. "The details would drive me insane."

"Get your thumb out of my ass."

He fisted a hand in my hair. "Would you rather I give you my cock instead?"

"You can take your cock and your lies and shove them up your ass, Gage."

"I'll forgive your verbal rampage. I know how pregnancy hormones can make a woman crazy."

"I'll show you crazy!" I struggled atop his lap, kicking my feet and tipping precariously head-first toward the floor. He tugged me back into position by the hair, and it became clear that no matter what I did or said, he wouldn't dislodge that thumb until he was ready. "Let me go."

"No," he said. "We're going to sit here like this until you calm down and find a little rationality. I understand you're angry, but you're reacting like this because of hormones."

"Stop pretending you know me better than I know myself! Katherine busted your lies wide open, Gage. You can't just wash it away like it never happened. You didn't fuck her for months—you fucked her for years! You put a goddamn ring on it."

"We were engaged for a few months, and those months were a mistake."

"Why were they a mistake?"

"Because I didn't love her."

"You used her."

"I'm a bastard, so yes. I admit it."

"Just like you used me." The fight seeped from my tired bones, leaving me limp on his lap. "Am I just a conquest to you? Do you love me at all?"

He withdrew his thumb and pushed me to my feet. "I'm going to pretend you didn't just ask me that."

I stumbled back, heeding the reminder of my sore ass as cause to keep my distance. "Don't you think it's time we stopped pretending? How can I trust you after you kept something so momentous from me? Did you put my ring on her finger?" I thrust my left hand toward him, displaying the large diamond that had once belonged to his mother.

He dropped his head and dragged both hands through his thick hair. "Of course not."

"I don't understand," I said. "Why ask her to marry you?"

"Fuck, Kayla. I don't know, okay? I have no answers for you. You think I'm a mess now? You should have seen me back then. She was the closest thing I had to Liz."

A sob caught in my throat. "She still is." I whirled and headed for the door, but everything blurred through my tears. As I reached for the knob, he shot out a hand to stop me.

His powerful form brushed my back, and I sensed the rapid rise and fall of his chest. "Don't go. She doesn't matter."

"If she didn't matter she wouldn't be standing between us."

"The only thing standing between us is your doubt."

Closing my eyes for a few moments, I sucked in a calming breath. "You kept her around, Gage. All of these years, she's been working for you. Even after we married, you kept her on your payroll."

"After today, she's gone."

"It's too little, too late."

"Don't say that, baby." He nuzzled my neck, breath hot on my skin. "I only kept her on because she threatened to to tell you shit I'd rather forget about."

That somehow made it even worse. She'd blackmailed him to keep her job. "Why were you so afraid to tell me?"

"I knew you'd take it wrong."

I turned the knob and pulled. He pushed.

"I'm taking it the way any *rational* woman would." Gritting my teeth, I yanked hard and got the door open by an inch. "Let me go, or I'll scream for Simone."

He backed away immediately, allowing me to slip into the hall. I rushed toward Simone, who would undoubtedly strengthen my resolve to put some distance between Gage and me. But with every stride of my trembling legs, I sensed him on my heels. The hold he had on me was undeniable, and it threatened to pull me back into that room and over his lap.

Hell, I'd probably spread my cheeks for him.

Simone rose from her perch near the edge of the living room, suitcase in hand. "Ready?"

To throw up? Maybe.

Unable to form words, I nodded.

Gage tangled our fingers together, holding me back while Simone escaped through the front door. "Watching you walk out that door is going to wreck me. You know that, right?"

I couldn't look at him—if I did, I'd crumble. "I need some space. Please, just let me go."

And I wondered how much it had cost him to let my fingers slip through his.

24. REUNIONS

"Hey, baby. Happy Thanksgiving! Are you having fun with gramps and gran?" Eve hadn't seen them in a year or so, other than the time they'd come down for her sixth birthday, so even though I hated sharing her with them on a holiday, they were her grandparents—the only ones she had left.

"We had lots of fun. They took me to the Space Needle yesterday! Did you know it's like the highest place *ever?*"

I closed my eyes, simultaneously cringing and celebrating how grown up she'd become. She was still my little girl, but she'd matured, possibly beyond her years, and she had opinions and ideas and dreams.

Thank God she hadn't developed an interest in boys yet.

"Have you ever been there, Mom?"

"Nope. We'll have to go sometime. I'm sure Gage—"

I shot a stricken look at Simone, who returned my stare with a sympathetic tilt of her mouth.

"Listen, I'm so happy you're having fun, but I'm gonna let you go so you can spend some time with your grandparents. Tell them I said Happy Thanksgiving."

"Okay! I love you," she said.

"Love you too. See you on Sunday."

With a sigh, I handed Simone her phone. "She's going to be devastated, unless…"

Simone shook her head. "Give yourself a day or two, then figure out what you're going to do. Maybe you'll be back in the devil's lair by then…" She halted upon my scowl. "Or maybe not. Either way, teleport across that bridge when you get to it."

How she managed to turn my scowl into laughter was beyond me. "What do you need help with?"

She quirked a brow. "Only everything. I kinda suck at cooking. I managed to get the turkey stuffed and in the oven."

"Good thing I'm here then." We got to work, and as I peeled potatoes, she chattered about some relationship drama at the hospital between a doctor and a head nurse. But she was also trying to follow the directions on putting together a green bean casserole. Watching her multitask was entertaining, and a little scary when she almost dumped in too much cream of mushroom soup.

"Jeez, Simone. I think you need to take a breather."

She plopped onto a barstool. "I'm sorry. I'm just really fucking nervous right now."

"How come?"

"Because I invited Ian."

The peeler stalled in my hand. "Oh, well…that makes

sense. You guys are dating now, so why shouldn't you spend the holiday together?" As I resumed peeling the last potato, I didn't have to peek at her from the corner of my eye to know she was studying me.

Rising from the stool, she crossed to the oven and checked on the turkey. "Are you sure about this? I was your friend long before his…"

"You can say it, Simone. I'm not going to burst into pregnant tears, I swear."

Closing the oven, she afforded me a sheepish smile. "Just checking. You're already in enough turmoil. I don't want to make it worse."

"You're my friend. My *best* friend, in fact. And he's Gage's brother, *soo*…" I said, moving the pot of peeled spuds onto the stovetop. "This is something I'm just going to have to get used to." Needing to keep busy, I rinsed the few dishes that had collected in the sink before stashing them away in the dishwasher.

"You think you'll be able to work shit out with Gage?"

"I hope so." I propped against the counter and let my hands dangle over the sink. "Maybe I made a huge mistake by leaving." If he knew I was about to spend the holiday with not only Simone but Ian too, he'd blow a gasket. But after the dirt Katherine had spilled, I couldn't bring myself to care.

"I don't think you made a mistake at all. He kept a huge part of his life from you while demanding you give him everything. That's pretty fucked up."

"That's Gage," I said, a note of tender sadness

strangling my words.

Simone sighed. "I'm not blind. You'll go back, probably before the turkey's done. But Sometimes, a girl's gotta breathe. Especially with you being pregnant. A little time to deal and process won't hurt anyone."

She made perfect sense. It was a talent of hers. But usually, her logic defied my heart's, because my bleeding organ beat for Gage.

Except it skipped a treacherous beat upon the knock that sounded. Simone rushed through her moderate-sized apartment and flung the door open. I remained motionless in the background, unnoticed as Ian drew her into his arms and planted one on her lips.

I wouldn't lie, least of all to myself. Seeing him with someone else wasn't the easiest thing in the world, but I couldn't stop the curve of my lips at witnessing how happy he seemed.

Or how head-over-heels Simone was for the man who'd at one time held my heart in his gentle hands. I'd returned his kindness and devotion by ripping him to shreds. But she'd weaved him back together, and I refused to let my drama get in the way of that, or ruin this holiday.

Simone broke away as Ian shut the door, but his hazel eyes widened upon the sight of me standing just outside the kitchen, wringing my hands because I didn't know what else to do with them.

"Hi…" His surprise registered in his deep voice.

"Hi," I said, my cheeks heating from the sudden awkwardness in the room. I looked to Simone for help.

"Kayla's spending Thanksgiving with us," she rushed to explain.

Ian took a step toward me. "Are you okay? Where's Gage?"

"He and I are...taking a break."

The astonishment that washed his face attested to the momentous nature of my news, and it told me how bad of an idea being the third wheel was. I moved to grab my coat. "I shouldn't be here. This is just..."

Way beyond awkward.

I had one arm in my jacket sleeve before Ian placed his hand on my shoulder. "Don't go. You're always welcome." He glanced at Simone, including her in the conversation. "Right, babe?"

So they were at the "babe" stage. I wondered how much time they'd spent together. Had Simone visited him at the treatment center, wherever that had been? Just how long had he been back?

And that's when I realized there were things I'd probably never know, and for a good reason too, because our histories were cocooned in hurt, and crisscrossed in a web of wrong. We only had two options at this point; remain hung up on the past, or salvage what little friendship we had left.

The third choice—walk away for good—was unfathomable.

Simone gave me a reassuring smile, so I assumed she voted for the second option. "Of course she's welcome. We're all adults, but more importantly, we're friends."

My husband excluded, for obvious reasons.

Ian removed his jacket, and we settled in to watch parts of the *Macy's Thanksgiving Day Parade* while the food cooked and boiled. When it came time to carve the turkey, Ian took on that task as I set the table for three. With each minute that passed, the nagging awkwardness subsided. We settled around a table crammed full of turkey and all the trimmings. I loaded up my plate, overjoyed that my morning sickness was mostly a thing of the past since I'd entered the second trimester.

"How about we say what we're thankful for?" Simone arched a brow at me. "Would you like to go first?"

I set down my eggnog with a slight gulp. "Um, sure. I'm grateful for…"

The baby.

But thinking about my unborn child brought tears to my eyes, and I didn't know if Ian was aware of my pregnancy. The last thing I wanted was to rub it in his face.

"I'm grateful for your unconditional friendship." My gaze swerved between the two of them. "Both of you. You've been there for me, each in different ways, for such a long time. So that's what I'm thankful for."

Simone took Ian's hand. "You're next."

"I'm gonna have to cheat and mention two things. I'm grateful to be alive." He brought her hand to his lips. "And I'm grateful for you."

Silence fell over the table, neither comfortable nor uncomfortable. It just was.

Simone cleared her throat. "I'm grateful for the three kids whose cancer went into remission this week. By the grace of God, they got to go home and spend the holiday with their families."

I raised my glass. "That takes the cake, Simone. It deserves a toast." Our glasses clinked together—three glasses representing three lives that had come together through trial and tribulation, yet here we were, sitting around the same table and thankful to do so.

But God, how I missed Gage just then. And Eve. Frigid air whistled through the holes in my heart where they should have been. With a little distance, I saw things more clearly, and Gage's past with Katherine didn't lance my heart as badly as it had yesterday. But not being with him did.

A bang on the door went off like an omen as if the universe heard my pain and wanted to reply. Even so, dread formed in my gut. I didn't know how I knew, but that angry fist pounding on Simone's door belonged to Gage.

She scooted back, the legs of her chair scraping loudly across her floor. "I'll deal with it, Kayla."

Except that I beat her to the door. She tried stopping me from opening it, but nothing and no one would keep me from seeing him. The instant I laid eyes on his disheveled appearance—his uncombed hair and the redness that rimmed his eyes—I fought against myself to fall at his feet.

He barreled into Simone's apartment, letting the door slam behind him. Everyone seemed to hold their breath for a few heavy seconds as Gage and Ian exchanged a look. But it wasn't a look I could put a name to.

"What are you doing here?" I asked.

"It's Thanksgiving, and my wife isn't at home. What do you think I'm doing here?"

Simone tried wedging between us—always the protector—but Ian gently held her back. He pulled her to his side, one hand curving around her shoulder, and Gage didn't miss the obvious bond they'd come to know in such a short time.

"I think you should leave," she said, though her tone was far from harsh. She might not like Gage, but she managed to rein in her temper for my sake because that's the type of friend she was—the type of friend who invited the ex-girlfriend of her new boyfriend to Thanksgiving.

"I'm not leaving without my wife."

"Gage, please don't do—"

"I mean it," he interrupted. "What do I need to do to get you to come home?" To my utter astonishment, he dropped to his knees and nuzzled my belly. "You want me to beg? Well here I am, baby. For you and our children, I'll do anything, even if it means getting on my knees, and I don't give a fuck who's around to see it."

God, I was going to cry.

"Gage, please get up." As much as I loved him kneeling at my feet, we both knew he didn't belong there. "I'll go home with you."

"You don't have to do that," Simone said.

Gage shot her a glare. "This is between my wife and me."

"Then why did she come to my house with a packed

suitcase? You need to give her some time."

"She's had time. Slumber party is over."

My friend was about to explode, so I interjected before she did. "Thanks for everything, Simone," I said, silently pleading with her to understand. "I think I should go home."

"But you were a mess yest—"

"Babe," Ian said, massaging her shoulders as if that would be enough to calm her. Who knew? Maybe it would. He probably knew her buttons and how to set off each one better than anyone. "Let them go. Kayla's a big girl. She can take care of herself."

His new attitude astounded me, and I couldn't help but wonder if a second chance at life was the only reason behind the change. I knew Gage had spoken to him the night he sent him away, but I'd never had the guts to ask what they'd talked about.

And I probably never would. That was a conversation Gage would likely never tell me about. We both had our flaws; I relapsed into the land of trust issues every time new doubts arose, and he refused to open up emotionally. We could fight each other on those two things until we destroyed our marriage and each other, or we could accept them.

Everyone had flaws. Some more than others.

"Thank you for having me," I said. Not everyone was lucky enough to be blessed with a friend like Simone. She'd always have my back, and I prayed that when the time came, if it ever did, I'd get a chance to have hers as well.

Gage laced our fingers together. "Where's your suitcase?"

"By the couch." I pointed to the sofa where I'd slept last night, tossing and turning and agonizing over my impetuous decision to leave. There was a saying I'd once read in some pregnancy book, or maybe I'd seen it on a forum, but I'd found the advice sound.

Never make big decisions while pregnant.

Gage fetched my suitcase as I put on my coat. Before we reached the door, I stopped to give Simone a hug. But I didn't dare touch Ian, and the glance he exchanged with Gage spoke volumes. Just because they'd managed to occupy the same room for ten minutes without tearing each other's heads off didn't mean they were on the way to becoming best buds.

But I was optimistic. People changed. Gage had, in spite of his habit of hiding painful things from his past. I had too, in spite of my penchant for doubting first and asking questions later. Even Ian had gone through a metamorphosis. Maybe, by some miracle, these two would someday bury the past and find some common ground.

We left without another word, having already said our goodbyes—for now anyway—and Gage pulled my luggage behind him as he led me to the car. After stowing the suitcase in the trunk, he opened the passenger door and helped me into the seat.

Gage settled in beside me and amped up the heater before digging my cell out of his pocket. "It still works," he said, handing it to me as if it were a token of apology.

GEMMA JAMES

"But I'm afraid the screen is cracked. We'll get you a new one."

I merely nodded, my thoughts still lingering on what had happened in Simone's apartment. Gage steered the car onto the road. Fog hung over the city, obscuring skeleton trees and roadway signs, and though the heater blasted warm air toward me, I shivered in my cold leather seat. Neither of us spoke until we were on the freeway.

"Did you know he was going to be there?" he asked.

"No."

A few nail-biting beats passed. "They seem happy together," he said.

I could not have given him a more stunned expression. "I think they are."

Letting out a breath, he ran irritated fingers through his messy hair. "I didn't sleep at all last night."

"Neither did I."

"Baby...I was wrong."

I had no words. My mouth was too busy gaping.

"I should have told you."

"I'm glad you can see that now," I said.

"But if you ever leave me like that again..." He shook his head, jaw rigid.

"So I'm to be punished then?"

"What do you think, Kayla?"

"Am I not allowed to have feelings?" I angled to face him head-on. "What about space? Is that out of the question too?"

"You're allowed to have feelings. But space? Fuck no. Not only are we married, but you belong to me. If you need space, I'm happy to put you in the cage for a while. You can have all the time in the world to think things through in there."

I gulped. "Gage, please."

"Please, what?"

"Please don't hate me for what I did."

He glanced at me, raising incredulous brows. "That's not even possible. Jesus, Kayla. I'm upset that you bolted like that, but I don't hate you. I could never *hate* you. I'm so fucking in love with you that I can't see straight."

"You might want to tone down the love a little, so you don't wreck the car."

He laughed. "Fuck, you're crazy, and I love you for it."

"When she told me those things, I *went* crazy, and I doubted you. *Again*. This nasty voice in my head told me you only wanted me to get at him, that I'm only a possession to you. A thing you use."

"You're everything to me."

On that note, with those words echoing in my mind in the soft way he'd spoken them, we rode the rest of the way home in silence. By the time we reached the driveway and rushed to the front steps, the sky had opened, but we beat the worst of it by seconds. Rain pounded the windows and danced on the rooftop.

And something smelled delicious. My stomach growled, reminding me that Gage's arrival had interrupted dinner.

"Come," he said, reaching for my hand. He escorted me into the dining room where a man I'd never seen before readied the table for us. A full Thanksgiving dinner had been set out.

"Dinner is served, Mr. Channing. Do you require anything else?"

"No, thank you."

The man made himself scarce, and a couple of moments later, I detected the front door open and close.

"You knew I'd come back."

"I was hoping." His mouth tilted up in a halfway grin. Bringing a hand to his tie, he loosened the knot before reaching into his pocket. "First things first though." He fisted a set of clover clamps—the worst kind I'd ever been punished with.

"If you weren't pregnant, you'd have a date with my bullwhip in the anal stocks right now. Lucky for you," he said, coming closer, "your womb is growing my baby and making your belly sexy as fuck." Stopping in front of me, he cocked his head to the side. "Just how sensitive are your nipples these days?"

I covered my breasts on instinct until he flattened his mouth into a firm line. Slowly, I let my hands drop and dangle at my sides.

"Good girl," he said, beginning with my left nipple.

"Ow!"

"It hurts, does it?"

"What do you think?" I said, scowling.

"Good. Now address me properly before I change my mind about the stocks." He raised a thoughtful brow. "Or you could spend some time in the cage after dinner."

"No, Master. Please. I'll be good."

"It is Thanksgiving, and I'm feeling grateful and a bit lenient, so assuming you get rid of that bratty attitude and let me feed you," he said, pinching my other nipple between his horrible clamp, "I'll offer you some mercy. No cage."

I was relieved to hear the words *no cage* fall from his lips, but my mind had latched onto the first part of what he'd said. "Feed me, Master?"

"Mmm, yes." He whirled me around, causing my head to spin, and used his tie to bind my hands at the small of my back. "I imagine you'll have a difficult time eating without the use of your hands." Happy with his handiwork, he pushed me into a chair and ordered me to spread my legs before taking a seat a mere arm's length away.

And in between bites of turkey, mashed potatoes and gravy, and the best damn cranberry sauce I'd ever had, he fingered my pussy until I teetered on the edge of orgasm, then he yanked on the chain connecting the clamps every time I uttered a plea to come, no matter how small. Even a whimper for more got my nipples punished. My face had become a tear-stained mess from the vises trapping my overly sensitive buds in never ending torture. And yet the pain faded the instant he pushed his fingers into me again.

Arching my spine, I curled my toes. "Please let me come!"

He brought those same digits, slick with my arousal, to my chin. "You will not come tonight."

I groaned.

"But you'll be happy about something else." Turning intense blue eyes on me, he slowly dipped his fingers between my lips. "The next time you do come, it'll be at the expense of the bitch who made you leave me in the first place."

25. KARMA'S TORTURE

I stood inside the bathroom in the basement and listened to the thump of footsteps on the stairs. A few seconds later, Gage's voice filled the space, his tone arrogant and authoritative. I hated that tone of his, but I hated that he was using it with *her* even more.

Katherine. The bitch who'd nearly torn my marriage apart by preying on my insecurities. That whole *fool me once* phrase echoed through my mind, and I chewed over how it fit me perfectly.

"You'll park your ass against that cross because I said so. Don't make me change my mind about this," he said.

"Where's your wife?" The racket of her heels faded away from where I hid. "Is she out shopping for groceries?" Her laughter got under my skin. "Or maybe she's at a bake sale."

"That is why I'm going to gag your irritating mouth."

"But I want to suck your—" A muffled whine cut her off, mid-sentence.

"See?" he said. "That's one thing you never

understood about me." Chains clinked, and I could almost hear the cuffs locking her wrists and ankles in place. "I don't care about your wants."

Creeping closer to the entrance, I waited for my cue.

"Kayla understands though. She knows and accepts that her wants come second to mine."

A few seconds later, Gage called for me to come out of hiding. I stepped into the main part of the basement, my own four-inch heels noisy on the floor, and the look on Katherine's face was one I wanted to catalog and pull out to gawk at for years to come. Six months ago, I'd been in her place, chained to the St. Andrew's cross and silenced with a gag, while Gage taunted me with his hard cock and her eager mouth.

Turnabout was fair play, and it tasted sweeter than ever.

Straining against her bindings, she attempted to shout epithets around the ball of rubber stretching her lips.

"I said I wanted to fuck, and you couldn't wait to get over here, could you?" he said to her, tilting his head as he held an arm out toward me. I fit at his side like I belonged, and I couldn't imagine ever leaving my place again. "I never said who I was going to fuck."

Katherine shook her head, a desperate whine emanating from her throat, but her eyes spit venom. Gage crossed to her fully-clothed body and grabbed her chin. "If you ever come near my wife again, a little bondage and humiliation will be the least of your worries."

Gage turned his back on her, but when I met his eyes, longing sparked between us. And Katherine? For a few intense moments, she failed to exist. I parted my lips, standing like a pillar to keep from pressing my thighs together. Only a couple of days had passed since we'd torn up the sheets.

But I was ravenous, hungry to feel him inside me, and the bed a few feet away called like a siren at sea. I couldn't wait to rock it.

"Take your dress off," he said, his feet slowly bringing him toward me.

Katherine's angry protests grew louder. As I reached behind my back and pulled the zipper down, I threw her a triumphant look.

"Eyes on me," he ordered.

The dress slid down my body, pooling around my feet. "Yes, Master."

"She doesn't matter." There was a double meaning in his statement. "Say it, Kayla."

"She doesn't matter."

He lifted a hand and drew a line between my breasts. "Right now, the only one who matters is me." Leaning forward, he teased my mouth with his lips. "Only me, baby."

I ached to kiss him, to undress him, to do *something*. But I did nothing. He gave me one night a year to take the lead, and tonight wasn't it.

He led me to the bed and pushed on my shoulders until I sat on the edge, then he brought my hands to his buttons. I undid each one in haste, my fingers jittery yet eager to remove the barrier of his clothing. His shirt parted, and I couldn't help but smooth my palms over his warm skin. His stomach muscles quivered under my touch, making him hiss in a breath.

"I love your hands on me."

Katherine's muffled words drew my attention to the cross, but Gage palmed my cheek and brought my gaze back to him. "If you look at her again, I won't let you come."

The idea just about destroyed me. "I'll be good, Master," I whispered.

"That's my girl." He shrugged out of his shirt and let it drift to the floor. "Lay back and spread your legs.

As I reclined on the mattress, heels pressing into the comforter, he reached for the button of his pants. But watching him shed the rest of his clothing put me in too precarious of a position, as Katherine struggled to get free just to the left of Gage, and she was doing her best to grab my attention.

Even rendered powerless, she still believed she could drive a wedge between Gage and me.

Letting my legs drape to the sides, I focused on the ceiling and tuned her out. The mattress dipped, and he grasped my inner thighs, gently pushing, opening me wider to the heat of his gaze. A hot tingle rippled through me. God, his touch alone was enough to flood my pussy with want.

"Master," I moaned, shuddering. I was about two days past due for my next fix.

"So wet," he murmured, his breath making me even wetter. "Are you going to be a good girl?"

I wanted to behave more than anything, but my grasp

on control slipped by the second. "Master, please. I want to be good."

"You want to come."

"I want you inside me."

"Trust me, baby. My cock wants inside you too. But first I'm going to lick you for a very long time, and you will *not* come. Do you understand me?"

I rolled my head back and forth on the mattress. "Don't do this to me. I can't take it."

"Yes, you can."

And then he lowered his mouth to my clit, teasing with gentle closed-mouthed kisses at first. I grabbed the bedding in both hands, thighs trembling from the overload of sensation. I was pathetic. He'd barely touched me, but I was ready to fly apart under his cruel mouth.

That cruel, sadistic, sexy mouth that went to work in driving me higher. He whirled his tongue, teased with his teeth, and when he lodged his thumb into my ass, I knew the gesture was far from a punishment. He had me squirming, moaning, begging, and crying tears of frustration for having to hold back for what seemed like an endless session of oral pleasure-turned-torture.

I lost track of time and space and reality. He'd dropped me in a realm where my pussy and his mouth were the only two things in existence. Eventually, I fell through the cracks and throbbed in suspension, my entire being aching for him to fill me.

"Master, please!"

He slid his palms over the gentle swell of my belly before settling on my breasts, and the friction of his hands pebbled my nipples. He climbed onto the mattress and entered me with a forceful thrust that declared his ownership.

And I came.

"Oh God!" Clawing at his shoulders, I held on and rode the wave. "Please don't punish me."

"Shh," he said, nipping my lips. "You're beautiful when you shatter. I want to watch you come again."

As our bodies locked together, he dragged me to that otherworldly high again, cock plundering me to orgasm after orgasm. His thrusts were manic, partly driven by the need to show Katherine that we were made for each other.

But his ultimate end game was to make me cry, "No more, Master!"

This level of exquisite torture wouldn't be complete without first driving me to beg for it, then making me plead for it to stop. Even then, he launched me deeper into madness. This crazed man wouldn't stop fucking me until he was good and ready.

Exhausted, I lay beneath his thrusting body, limp with weakness and powerless to do anything but let him extract painful orgasms from me.

26. KARMA'S LAST LAUGH

As I came down gradually, silence descended over the basement like a protective fog that shielded us from the outside world. Every few seconds, a long, satisfied exhale would dent it.

But not break it.

We lay wrapped up in sweat and each other, loathe to fracture this moment, until Katherine let out a muffled screech, and the real world came pounding on our fortress.

Gage pressed his lips to mine for one last stolen kiss, then he slipped from the bed and reached for his pants. I sat up, hair falling into my eyes as he buttoned his slacks. He fetched my dress, and I didn't dare look at Katherine until I stood on solid ground again, fully clothed, even if my husband's cum dripped down my thighs underneath my skirt.

A sheen of hostility cast her face in red, and she'd balled her hands into fists so tight that they were nearly colorless. Doubt sank into my gut. Fucking my husband in front of her had been the best payback ever, but I worried we'd achieved little more than the sharpening of her claws.

Gage removed the gag from her drooling mouth.

"I'll have you arrested for this!" she shrieked.

"No, you won't." He freed her ankles and wrists before crossing to the nightstand next to the bed, where he kept smaller items like lube and nipple clamps inside the drawer. He withdrew a set of documents and thrust them into her shaking hands.

"What's this?"

"You've been served."

"What?" Pursing her lips, she shuffled through the papers. "What the hell is this?"

"Can't you read? It's a restraining order. You're not allowed within 500 feet of Kayla or our children. And since she's an employee of Channing Enterprises, with duties that may take her to any of the company's offices, you no longer work for me."

"On what grounds?"

He advanced on her until her back hit the wall. The papers fluttered to the floor around them in a disarrayed mess. I didn't like him anywhere near her, but I found a small amount of justice in the maneuver because she'd done the same thing to me a couple of days ago.

Only she'd put her hands on me. Gage didn't need to touch her to intimidate—not when the tense set of his jaw and the broadness of his shoulders did the job for him.

"You threatened my wife and unborn child," he said,

placing his left palm flat on the wall next to Katherine's head. "You barged into my home while drunk and put your fucking hands on my wife."

"I wasn't drunk, and I didn't touch her."

"Don't bother trying to lie about this. Kayla recorded your conversation, including your threats." He leaned forward, invading her space to the max, but he still refrained from touching her. "You can bet your ass I'll use it in court. If I had any reservations about going for full custody before, I don't now."

She shook her head, eyes glistening with tears. "You can't take my son from me."

"I didn't want to go this route, but you've caused nothing but trouble."

She dropped to her knees and grasped his pant legs. "I'll leave your wife alone. I promise. Please don't take my son from me!"

He moved out of reach, and she tipped forward, palms flat on the floor in the midst of strewn papers.

"Nothing you say will change my mind," he said. "Now get the fuck up and get out of my house." He bent and gathered the documents.

As Katherine rose to her feet, her expression hardened, and I expected her to go off on a tirade. Instead, she started laughing—a deep and smug sound that emanated from her belly. It was manic and disturbing on so many levels.

"You're as gullible as your wife." She yanked the documents from his hands. "I honestly don't know why I wasted so many years on you."

"The feeling's mutual. Now get the fuck out and don't come back. I won't allow you to fuck up my marriage anymore, and as for Conner, I'll do what I have to do to protect him from you."

Her lips curved in pure viscousness. "He's not your son."

"Excuse me?"

She shrugged. "You're not the father."

"Of course I am!" Gage roared. "I have the paternity test to prove it."

She let out another laugh. "I wanted it to be you, but it's not, and you've made it clear tonight that it won't ever be."

"Why are you pulling this shit now?" His voice bellowed through the basement.

"Because you left me no choice! I wanted you to be the father, but I'll be damned if I let you take my son from me."

Gage clenched his teeth, but before he could unleash his anger, I entwined my fingers with his. Katherine had blindsided him with this, possibly to provoke him into doing something he'd regret.

He inhaled then let the breath out five seconds later. "We did a paternity test," he reminded her, his tone calmer than she deserved.

She shrugged. "You share DNA with the father, so that test gave a false positive. But Conner's not yours. It's impossible, based on the date of conception."

"Who *is* Conner's father then?" The question echoed off the walls, but he already knew the answer, same as I.

"Ian." She lowered her head, fingers thumbing the restraining order. "I slept with him a few weeks after you broke up with me."

"Why didn't you tell me? Or hell! Why didn't you tell Ian? You fucked with Conner's head for years."

"Because I wanted you back!" she shouted. "If you'd known I'd gotten knocked up by your brother…? C'mon, Gage. We both know you would have never spoken to me again."

"Ain't that the truth."

"Ain't that poetic justice." She folded the papers and gripped them in both hands. "I have more in common with Liz that you ever knew. Your brother knocked us both up." She headed for the stairs, and Gage worked his jaw, watching in a state of anger and shock and disbelief as she climbed to the top.

"I guess that makes you his problem then!"

The door slammed shut, leaving us in the wreckage of a plan that had backfired horribly. Gage pushed his hands through his hair, breathing hard, but when his eyes met mine, that was my undoing. I crossed to him, but he slid to the floor before I could touch him.

"He's not my son."

Falling to my knees in front of him, I wedged between his legs and grabbed his face. His eyes glassed over with tears, and one slipped free, hanging on his lashes before dripping down his cheek. I brushed it away, wishing I could wipe away the devastation I saw in the slump of his shoulders and the sheen of his eyes.

"He's not my son," he repeated as if saying it again

would make it sink in. "But I love him like my own."

"I know." I had no words to take away his pain, so I wound my arms around him and held on. Getting through this seemed impossible just then, but we were stronger together, and I knew we'd find a way to overcome Katherine's final curveball.

27. THE DEVIL'S GRACE

Five and a half months later...

"I fucking hate you!" Holding Gage's hand with enough force to crush bones, I screamed through another contraction. I was certain his fingertips had gone white, cut off from blood flow by my unnatural grip, but he didn't seem to care. Using his free hand, he wiped the sweat from my brow.

"You're almost there, baby."

"I'm hurting you," I groaned, squeezing tears from my eyes. They dripped down my flushed face. "Your fingers..."

"It's okay. I'm not going anywhere. I'm right here." As if to get his point across, he rubbed a thumb over the back of my hand.

The horrid peak of the contraction subsided, and I collapsed against the pillows, trying to catch my breath. How was I supposed to push a baby out when I had no strength left? I hadn't given birth in over six years. Funny how time had a way of erasing just how fucking insane women were for going through this again and again and again.

Fucking loons.

Forty seconds later, another contraction began the climb to agony, and I looked at Gage, tightening my jaw in panic.

"Oh no…another one…"

Through the pain and delirium, some part of my mind acknowledged they were coming faster and harder…that was a good thing, right?

No! Fucking make it stop. Make. It. Stop.

The pain was…I had no words for this level of torture. Nothing Gage had subjected me to had ever hurt this badly. Each contraction brought me closer to meeting our baby for the first time, but it was hell—an endless sentence to purgatory where a vise stronger than anything known to man clamped and squeezed and pulverized from the inside. I grabbed hold of the bedside rail, certain the power of my grip would shake that fucker to pieces.

"I can't do this!" I said in a high-pitched shriek. "Oh God, Gage. I'm scared!" Wrenching my hand from his, I scooted to my side and clutched the railing with both fists. Pressure built between my thighs, rushing faster until it settled low in my womb. Instinctively, I lifted a leg, and Gage wound a strong arm under my thigh to prop me up.

Because I couldn't do it on my own.

He pushed strangled locks of hair from my cheeks.

"You're doing amazing."

"I think she's coming."

"She, huh?"

We'd decided to keep the sex of our baby a surprise, but I'd had dreams, and as crazy as it might sound, I was positive the universe had given me signs. Like the time we'd gone shopping for Eve's Christmas presents and a pink sippy cup had somehow ended up in the cart. Deep down, I knew the baby was a girl. I didn't need an ultrasound to confirm what my heart already knew.

"Yeah, she. And she's coming...fuck...oh *fuck*..." The bed rail became my birthing partner, and I gave it another shuddering assault before collapsing again. "Where's the doctor? I think I need...I need to push!"

Gage cursed under his breath. "The nurse was here a few minutes ago. As for the doctor..." He searched the room. "Baby, you can't push yet."

"Don't you think I'd stop if I could?" I shouted, glowering at him, wishing *he* was the one going through this.

He jabbed the call button a dozen or so times, but it didn't matter. She was coming, and she wasn't waiting.

"Gage..."

"Hold on, baby. I'm trying to get—"

"Gage!" Something unnatural hurtled from my lungs —a cross between a howl and a grunt. It was purely animalistic. In that moment, as my baby moved down the birth canal, I felt like an animal.

Wild, uninhibited, and human in the basest form.

A flurry of motion erupted in the room. Dr. Keenan

rushed in, pulling gloves on in a hasty manner as a nurse readied the bed for delivery. Gage took my hand again, murmuring encouraging nothings.

I was in my own dimension, already pushing, despite the world not being ready for this child to be born. She was coming. *She* was ready, zooming to her first breath of air on her own terms.

"Doctor, she's crowning."

I glanced up at Gage and watched in complete awe as a tear slid down his cheek. During a break between pushes, I brought his hand to my mouth. "I'm sorry. I didn't mean it."

"Didn't mean what?"

"When I said I hated you."

"It's okay. You're allowed to say whatever you want right now."

More pressure built, stronger than ever, and as I grunted, powerless to do anything except let my body do its job, I managed to groan a question.

"What should we"—another long howl burst from my throat—"name her?"

And he chuckled through his tears, a sound as pleasant as wind chimes, or as comforting as rain on the rooftop. His laughter soothed my soul.

"She *or* he…you pick the name. You should definitely have the honor."

Bearing down again, I knew this was it. I'd never forget the way our child's tiny body slid from mine, or how the sound of that first cry was the sweetest thing I'd heard since Eve was born.

Our baby arrived on the eighth of May at 11:28 a.m.

Squalling the music of life.

Warming my belly and my heart.

Perfectly healthy with ten fingers and just as many toes. I knew because Gage counted.

Oh, and I was right. We were the proud and exhausted and overjoyed parents of a little girl.

When Gage held her for the first time—swaddled in a customary striped hospital blanket—and cooed about how special she was, and how he couldn't wait for her to meet her big sister, Eve and cousin Conner, that's when her name came to me.

"Grace," I said, barely above a whisper.

"Grace?"

"Her name. It's Grace."·

He treated me to a devastating smile, accompanied by a flash of his indigo eyes. "Fits her perfectly."

Acknowledgments

I have so many people to thank that I'm sure I'll forget someone, but here goes. First, I want to thank my family. They put up with my neurotic ways better than most would. If it weren't for the support of my husband, kids, and my mom this book wouldn't have seen the light of day.

And speaking of support teams, I've got to give props to a few beta readers/awesome pimpers. Rachel, who read huge chunks of this book last minute and made me laugh in PM's on Facebook as we traded obscene jokes (there might have been a picture too!). I've just gotta say that I appreciate you so much, and I'm stoked that I got to meet you in Chicago this year. Same to Deb. Woman, you rock! If I ever set foot in Florida again, it'll probably be because you've promised to meet me there with your snarky sense of humor (which I love), and a bottle of booze. And speaking of Florida, I had the absolute pleasure of meeting a reader at a signing this year. She and I spent a whirlwind of an evening together, talking books and life in general. Ashley, you have no idea how much that night meant to me. I can't thank you enough for our long chat in person, or the chats we've had since on social media.

Finally, to the readers, especially those that have followed Gage and Kayla from the beginning. This book wouldn't have happened without you. Whether you're Team Love-To-Love-Gage or Team Love-To-Hate-Gage, I LOVE you all! The words "Thank you" just aren't strong enough to convey how much I appreciate your support.

About the Author

Gemma James is a USA Today bestselling author of a blend of genres, from new adult contemporary to dark romance. She loves to explore the darker side of human nature in her fiction, and she's morbidly curious about anything dark and edgy, from deviant sex to serial killers. Readers have described her stories as being "not for the faint of heart."

She warns you to heed their words! Her playground isn't full of rainbows and kittens, though she likes both. She lives in middle-of-nowhere Oregon with her husband, two children, and a gaggle of animals.

For more information on available titles, please visit www.authorgemmajames.com

Made in the USA
Las Vegas, NV
22 March 2023

69512746R00132